AGAINST THE GRAIN

PLANTED AND PLOWED
BOOK 1

LAINEY DAVIS

ABOUT THIS BOOK

I've spent my whole life as an outsider, a man bound by rules and social norms I don't understand.

But there's one truth I definitely grasp: Eila Storm is the one for me.

She's wild and unpredictable and that usually sends me into a tailspin, yet I'm drawn to her like rain to a drainpipe. Eila gets me in a way nobody ever has, but she's also chaos incarnate—determined to start an urban farm on an abandoned lot ... without permits.

The problem? Once I know she never filed the paperwork, I can't look away. I don't know how to turn off my rigid need to follow the rules, even if that means shutting down her business.

She says I'm choking her like a weed. So how

can I let things go to earn her trust? She super-charges my central nervous system when I'm usually allergic to surprise. I crave her fiery passion more than the comfort of standard operating procedures.

I just need a little help to rewrite my own code so I can wrap Eila in understanding...and my arms.

A buttoned-up inspector falls for his polar opposite in Against the Grain, *book one of the Planted and Plowed series of romantic comedies starring the Storm sisters. Love takes roots in the cracks of life's pavement and stems get spliced in these steamy books full of small-town swoon in a big city setting.*

1

EILA

I DIDN'T LIKE that job anyway.

It's going to be fine.

Everything is different this time—I've got a good plan, and it's going to work. I just need to convince my sisters...and a whole bunch of other people.

But my sisters are the easiest, so I gathered most of them at our favorite dive bar for post-work drinks on sticky chairs, with sticky tables, and a damned good ceiling fan.

Eden, who's just ten months younger than me and my closest confidant, bites her lip and shakes the ice in her rum and Coke. "Are you sure you don't want to ask Esther for a job at her bar?"

I shake my head. The last thing I want to do is go crawling to our oldest sister looking for work. She'd want to analyze what happened at my last job and workshop my soft skills or something.

Eden sighs. "Explain it all to me again."

I sigh back at her and try to smooth out the paper where I took my frenzied notes. "We're going to take over the abandoned lot next door and plant hops there. We will then sell the hops."

Eliza wrinkles her nose. "Sounds illegal."

I wave a hand at this. "Who checks on the abandoned lots?" Eden and I live next to a ramshackle strip of land that gets excellent sun. It also gets excellent truckloads full of tires and weird garbage. I'm guessing from contractors who don't want to pay for commercial waste removal. "If we clean up the lot and plant shit there, people will stop using it as a dump site. Think of the earth!"

My sisters don't seem convinced. Probably because they haven't been obsessing about this for months like I have.

Eliza frowns. "Why hops, though? Since when is that a cash crop?"

I huff at her. "You run an urban goat business and you seem financially independent."

She tips her glass at me to acknowledge my point and I smile. I mean, she's not wrong—hops aren't the first thing that springs to mind when I envision a lucrative business model. But it's not like I have the license required for medical marijuana, so I picked the next best vice.

"We don't need to be millionaires. We just want to be stable, right?"

Eva, the youngest, arches a dark brow as she slurps at her screwdriver. "What's all this *we*? I don't want to be involved."

I wave this comment aside. "Me. I want to be stable. But, you know, I'll always be there for all of you. Once I can afford it."

Eden pats my hand. "We know, Eila. And, same. As you know. But ... hops? It's weird."

"It's no weirder than keeping bees or goats in the city." My sisters roll their eyes. "I've done a lot of research on this."

I hate working for other people. They always wind up trying to screw me over, whether it's giving me the worst shifts or stealing tips. I'm ready for my *own* business and this one will combine all my expertise: plants and beer. "The hops will grow pretty much anywhere. I've been doing recon on that farm up in Slippery Rock."

Eden gestures for me to continue, droplets of condensation from her drink splashing onto my manifesto, smearing the faint pencil lines even more than the pocket of my overalls, where the paper had been shoved all day.

My sisters are my entire support network, and

we're tight. If they disapprove of something I'm doing, I'll feel that impact every second of every day. Eden and I moved into our own place over a year ago, but I still feel a bit unmoored. Or maybe I feel too moored? Our oldest sister basically raised us, but living in Esther's house was tough. It always felt like she had more chores to hand out than hugs. But who needs hugs, really?

I'm in a serious relationship with plants; I just haven't quite managed to turn that hobby into anything more lucrative than the retail and nursery jobs I cycle through like toilet paper.

I tap the paper with my plans. "The way it works is it takes three years for the plants to mature. I'm sure the soil is crappy now, but the roots and leaves will absorb all the bad shit and it won't transfer through to the hops' cones. I'm telling you the research shakes out."

Eliza squints through the smudges at the rough numbers I scrawled on the bottom of the page. "You really think you can sell a crop of hops for that amount? To a brewery here?"

I roll my eyes at her, a leftover teenage habit I can't seem to shake. "In three years when the plants mature, yeah. There's a big push for *buy local*. You see it everywhere. I see it every weekend at the market." Saw, I guess. I don't work there anymore.

My sisters nod. Eden especially. "People do love local honey." Eden keeps bees in our back yard.

I pump my fist in solidarity. "Hell yeah, they do. Look, you don't even have to do anything. I will clean up that vacant lot next to our house, I'll plant the hops, and your bees can pollinate them or whatever."

Eden only meant to have one hive, but she keeps getting called in to remove swarms of honeybees from people's property and she's running out of places to take the bees. Last I checked we had four hives out back.

"The hops repel mites. I'm telling you. Everyone wins!"

Eliza shrugs. "I have no horse in this race. Me and my goats are doing just fine, thank you. With permits."

I flick up my middle finger at her and start to fold the paper. "I can't keep working multiple jobs while I figure out my life."

Eliza squints and says, "Aren't we here because you currently don't have any jobs?"

I flip her the bird again.

Eden pats my hand. "Why don't you sign on with the medical marijuana farmers from your program?"

Eliza laughs, but it's not really a joke. Half the people I graduated horticulture school with are making bank tending ganja crops. The truth is that they didn't invite me to join them, and they had to pay big bucks for all the licensures. As per usual, I was left behind by the people around me who were supposed to care. Except my sisters. They've never let me down, and they're the only ones. I sigh and reach for my drink, finding the glass empty.

Eden leans toward me and whisper-yells, "Hey, Eila. Don't turn around."

I contract all my muscles. "You can't just say that, Eden. Telling someone not to turn around makes them desperate to turn around."

She squeezes Eliza's arm and the two of them peer over my shoulder. "That frowny guy is totally staring at Eila, right?"

Eliza's eyes widen. "Oh, totally." She tries to talk without moving her lips. "He doesn't even seem to care that we caught him."

I shake the glass again. "If there's a guy staring at me, he should at least buy me a drink."

I turn around in my seat and sure enough, there's a dark-haired guy looking at me intently above the top of his menu. "Someone should tell him not to bother with the menu here." I wave at him, and he pulls the menu up higher, covering his whole face.

Eliza kicks me under the table. "We should have gone to Esther's place for drinks."

"Since when can we afford to go to Bridges and Bitters?" Our big sister's bar serves high-end cocktails at a premium. "And don't tell me she'd let us drink free, because you know she'd make us work it all off scrubbing floors or something. Trust me, this is better."

I rise out of my seat, muscles groaning after a full day moving soil around at the plant nursery. Of course, they waited to fire me until after I worked a full shift.

I don't understand why anyone would be staring at me out of anything other than morbid curiosity. I reach up to my dark, messy bun, and sure enough, I have actual plants poking out of my knots. Whatever. Free drinks are free drinks.

I walk over to the guy. "Hey," I say, dropping into the chair opposite him. "You gonna just look at me in wonder or were you going to buy me a beer?"

He lowers the menu and blinks. "You like beer?"

I shrug. "Sure. Doesn't everyone like beer?"

He shakes his head rapidly. "No. Not at all. Most women seem to prefer wine. Or clear liquor." He looks at me intently. It's mildly uncomfortable, like he is trying to read my mind.

"Hm. Maybe. But I like beer. I'm a beer gal." I offer him my dirty, callused hand. "I'm Eila Storm."

He stares at my hand for a beat and then puts

his own callused hand into it, shaking exactly three times before retracting his arm. "Ben."

He doesn't really invite conversation, so I lean back in my chair, studying him. He's wearing a polo shirt and nice jeans with Timbs, but they're not dirty. So, he's obviously done manual labor in the past, just not in these clothes, today. "You live here in Garfield?"

My neighborhood has all kinds of people living here these days, but this guy doesn't strike me as the type to come from out of town and buy a flipped house sight unseen. I thought I detected a hint of a Pittsburgh accent.

He clears his throat. "Greenfield."

I smile at his reference to the blue-collar neighborhood, home to my favorite hockey bar. If possible, my smile seems to have made him stare even harder. "Well, Ben from Greenfield. Here in Garfield, it's customary to buy a girl a beer after you stare at her."

2

BEN

I know it's rude to stare. I managed to internalize that social rule at least. I also know I'm sending off "weird vibes," but I cannot look away from Eila Storm. Of course, her last name is Storm. She looks like she just finished wrestling a tornado. Eila has long, dark hair piled up on her head in a series of loops, each with tufts of grass and plant matter sticking out.

She's wearing overalls with nothing but a sports bra underneath, and her tanned skin is streaked with dirt.

I have never been more attracted to a woman before. Ever. I can't explain this at all.

I spend my days ensuring order and regulation. I inspect construction projects for the city, ticking off boxes and placing everything into neat columns. When something is as messy as Eila Storm, I reject it. Professionally. It's literally my job.

And here I sit with my mouth hanging open, soaking in this woman who keeps insisting I buy her a beer.

"Shit. Yes. I want to buy you a drink. What are you drinking?"

She lifts a brow and crosses her arms over my chest. "What am I drinking or what would I like? Because what I have is a half-cup of warm, shitty lite beer and what I'd *like* is the $8 new IPA with the Citra hops."

Oh crap she's throwing out options now. I clear my throat. "Which one should I buy you?"

She pauses and laughs. "That was confusing, wasn't it. New IPA, please. Let's sniff some hops."

I nod. "The Citra hops are amazing."

"Wait until you taste mine." Eila flicks the laminated menu currently stuck to the table in the humidity.

"You want me to taste your beer?"

She shakes her head again. "I have sort of a thing for hops. I'm growing some Cascade that will knock your socks off."

I understand her expression is an idiom--one I've learned and filed away--and I resist the urge to blurt that she herself has already knocked my socks off. "Did you say you grow hops?"

Eila nods. "Well. Sort of."

The server is hurrying between the rows of tables, and I nearly have to shout to get her attention. Which, of course, makes me anxious and she almost skitters away before I choke out, "my date wants a double IPA." I inhale and exhale rapidly, like I just heard bad news or something. "Please. When you get a chance. Thank you." I groan and sink a bit lower in my seat.

This is why I hardly go out. I can't even figure out how to order a beer without looking like a freak. I wish I'd just stopped at the grocery store for a six-pack after today's news. But then I wouldn't have lain eyes on this woman who smells like wood chips and sunshine.

She probably wonders why the weird guy is staring at her. But I'm not her. I'm me and all I can think about is the line of her collar bone where it intersects with the strap of her overalls.

Eila taps her hand on the table, causing it to wobble a bit. She's had ample opportunity to get up and walk away but hasn't. Maybe I'm not as much of a mess as I thought? "Are we on a date now?"

My cheeks heat. "I wasn't sure what sort of noun to use. It seemed strange to tell the server your name...I'm really bad at this."

She nods. "You are super bad at this."

She says this without judgment. Just stating facts. I like it. I crave this sort of person, who just says what they mean. I wonder if I should add this to the list of things to talk about with my new therapist. *How to find people who say what they mean.*

Eila finishes the bad beer in her cup and crushes the plastic, perhaps because she knows the more expensive beer is served in a nicer, tulip glass. Mess that she is, Eila seems to know and understand beer.

Beer people are usually much easier for me to be around. Even before I got officially diagnosed as Autistic, I knew there were certain categories of people who made me *less* uncomfortable than usual. If beer people are pretentious, it's about quality and craftsmanship and not as often about appearances or unspoken rules. Eila is open and expressive, even if she does use idioms.

The server sprints past, plunking Eila's drink on the table without a word. Eila perks up. "That was fast." She reaches for the glass and I watch, transfixed, as she sniffs it before drinking. I use this opportunity to study her eyes, noting flecks of brighter brown among the dark irises. She takes a tiny sip, taking her time and tasting the drink before swallowing. I watch her throat work and try not to imagine what it would feel like to lick that long column of skin.

Where are these thoughts even coming from? Perhaps I should indeed get out more often if this is all it takes to get my mind off this new piece of information I learned about myself.

"Man, that hits the spot. I've had a heck of a day, Stranger Ben."

I clear my throat and refocus my gaze on my own drink. "Oh?"

She nods. "I got fired." Eila takes a swig of her drink recounting the details of her day, which, like mine, began very early. "I'm not sure what I expected, working at a nursery, but apparently, I'm rude to the customers. People keep buying these awful imported plants that don't do well in our climate, and then they come back in and bitch that their flowers all died. Like...what did you expect planting hibiscus in Pennsylvania? *In the shade?*"

"People don't really like to read instructions." Where I find instructions crucial to moving through the day, most people view them as optional. I feel this very acutely with every property I inspect.

She waves a hand at me. "Thank you. It's infuriating." She takes another swig of beer. "Man, all I want to do is help people who *want* to learn more about plants. That's not true. I also want to sell hops to someone who can turn them into beer that tastes like this."

"This is a wonderful beer." I finish the last sip of

my glass and worry that there will be an awkward silence now while I figure out what to do with my hands, whether Eila plans to stay long enough for me to order another. There are a thousand movements and interactions to interpret as I remember why I don't like to leave my house. I'm surprised it took this long for me to learn I'm autistic. "So...you said you sort of grow hops?"

I've been seeing a therapist for a few months, and she suggested I look into an evaluation. It really didn't take long before the psychologist confirmed. I'm not sure why I feel like I got run over by a truck and simultaneously shown a world in full color for the first time.

So, I decided to go to a bar and process. And discovered Eila. This intriguing woman is the highlight of my year.

"Meh, it's a dream in progress. I promise I'll like it way better than slinging hostas but ... I do need to figure out something to earn an income for the time being." She exhales through her nose and takes another sip of her beer. I mirror her actions. "What about your day, Stranger Ben? Tell me something shitty that happened."

I lean back in my seat and purse my lips, considering. Do I tell her about today's diagnosis or stick to work topics like she started with? Today had been pretty run-of-the-mill before my appointment, which means a blend of projects done well and horror scenes. I must take longer than expected to answer, because Eila leans forward and presses her palms to the table. "This will be good. I can tell." I wince and she laughs. "No pressure. But keep in mind I explained why a customer couldn't grow avocados and then got fired for my tone, so that's your baseline."

Stick to work stories, got it. My mind zips to the first case of the day, an apartment remodel in Stanton Heights. "I had to explain why a shower and toilet shouldn't share a plumbing line." She laughs again, a loud guffaw of satisfaction. I feel like I've won a contest, getting her to emit that sound. Women don't laugh at my jokes, as a rule. Nobody can ever tell when I'm kidding.

"People are the worst."

I nod in agreement. She drinks her beer, and I start calculating how I can extend our time together. I should ask her for her number, right? To signal that I want to see her again ... I've just about landed on the perfect phrase when a pair of women approach Eila.

"We're heading out. You coming?"

She glances up at the women, one of whom puts a hand on her shoulder. They are all obviously related...sisters, perhaps? Eila nods and downs the rest of her beer in one gulp. "Yeah, give me one sec."

She smiles at me as her companions gather purses and sunglasses from their table. "Well, that's my ride. Thanks for the beer, Ben. And the commiseration."

She's gone before I can form words.

3

EILA

NONE of my relatives agreed to get up and help me this morning. Mondays are hallowed in my family. Almost all of us work in food service or retail, and all four of my sisters and I are off on Mondays. Of course, we're all the product of gross parental neglect so none of us knows how to sit still with our own thoughts or—you know—relax.

We always show up at Esther's house for family dinner on Mondays, even if family dinner is cereal and milk from one of Eliza's goats. The point is we're all there, together. Even Esther's husband is off on Mondays, since he coaches professional rugby, and they play their matches on weekends.

I guess my sisters draw the line at getting up early to help me haul trash from a potential tetanus minefield, though.

Everyone thought I was joking when I declared my intention to clean up this lot next to Eden's and my house. None of them agreed to lend a hand, although Eden said I could use her van if I found a place to take the garbage.

So, the way I see it, if none of them are going to help me physically, the least they can do is lend me space in their commercial Dumpsters. What's the point of Esther owning a bar if she can't share a little room in her trash bins?

I got up with the sun and spent a few hours with my T-Swift playlist, telling myself I'm in my "brown era" as I'm coated in dirt and filth. I don't mind getting dirty. I especially don't mind when it's a task I set, with my rules and my pace. The work goes fast, since a lot of the trash is already bagged from when the jerks threw it out their windows driving past our lot.

I load up the van before Eden emerges for breakfast and I sing my way to the alley behind Esther's bar.

The Dumpster is overflowing after just a few bags and I bite my lip, staring at the construction trash bin next door. This is a new addition to the back alley behind Bridges and Bitters, and from the sound of things, there's a gut job in progress in there.

Last year, some jerks lit the trash bins on fire,

causing the flames to spread to Esther's building. The space next door has been empty ever since then, but it seems like somebody finally decided to renovate.

I know it's illegal to throw trash in other people's commercial trash bins. Theft of services, they call it. I might have been cited for tossing a 40-ounce malt liquor bottle into one of those once when I was underaged. I decided I'd rather go down for theft of services than public intoxication plus underaged drinking plus whatever else they'd pile on.

I chew on the inside of my cheek, wondering if anyone is around to spy on the trash at nine on a Monday, when I see a familiar face emerge from the back door of Esther's neighboring building.

"Stranger Ben!" I wave at the guy from the bar the other night, still clutching the top of a black trash bag in one hand as I lean on the gritty Dumpster. "What are you doing here?"

He's taller than I imagined, which makes sense since I only saw him sitting down. Now, he is standing here wearing the hell out of a pair of khakis, I can't seem to look away from his long, lean form. Every bit of him seems taut, from his ass to his personality. His eyes widen as he takes me in and I watch as his focus darts between the bag in my hand, my face, and my chest, which is sweaty and wet in a clingy cut-off shirt I modified for better ventilation. Which is to say, it's pretty revealing. I adjust my shoulders, hoping this tucks my cleavage out of sight a bit.

"Eila Storm. What are *you* doing out here? You should have a hardhat on." He glances side to side, as if a rack of safety equipment will produce itself.

"Oh." I wave my free hand. "I'm just tossing out some trash for my sister. She owns Bridges and Bitters, and this is definitely her garbage for her Dumpster that she pays for."

Ben squints at the bag and I step a bit further from the construction Dumpster. "I know Esther Storm," he says, his voice even and low but his eyes suggesting he's met her on one of her fierce days.

I notice a City of Pittsburgh seal on his black polo shirt. "Do you work for the city? What are you doing in there *with* a hardhat on?"

The trash bag is getting sweaty in my hand I consider letting it go, but I'm worried it'll spill. I adjust my stance uncomfortably. Ben clears his throat and glances toward an official city vehicle now parked in. By me, via the van.

"I'm an inspector. Didn't I mention that the other night at the bar?"

My eyebrows shoot up and I clench my stomach. "Look, this really is my sister's trash bin. Honest."

Ben glances at the bag in my hand, which has begun to split a bit and some of the shingles emerge. "Is that roofing waste? What were you doing with that?"

I could feign offense and pretend he's accusing me of not being able to replace a roof due to my vagina. But he already knows I work with plants and that all my hobbies revolve around things closer to the ground. I sigh. "The vacant lot next to my house was full of all kinds of crap. People keep driving by and unloading. You should see all the tires I have... but I'm thinking of slicing those in half to make fencing or something..."

I drift off as Ben's face tightens. His eyes darken even more as I talk and I fear he's going to hit me with a clipboard or a citation. He breathes through his nose a bit and finally says, "Did you know the city has programs to help with waste removal from vacant lot cleanup?"

My eyes widen. "I did not know this. So, I wouldn't have had to haul all this crap here to Esther's garbage?"

He shakes his head. "If you give me the address, I can arrange for one of the smaller garbage trucks to come by. You'd just have to put the bags by the curb. Or by the road...if there is no curb left."

I grin at him. "Is this your way of asking for my number, Stranger Ben?"

He shakes his head rapidly. "No. I asked for your

address. But only for the trash removal. I would never impose."

I reach out to touch his arm, but he flinches. Which is totally fair because I'm filthy. "Hey, I was just teasing. I'd love you to send the trash truck. We're on Kinkaid, near Graham Street. There are a million steps, but no sidewalk left to speak of."

Ben nods as he clicks furiously on an official-looking iPad. I swallow, briefly concerned I've set myself up for scrutiny. I can't get a read on this guy. At the bar, he was obviously into me, but I didn't really give him a lot to go on, and I've caught him in his work environment. It makes sense that he'd be all business. Probably a good thing, since I don't have capacity for anything but business.

Ben looks up and flashes a smile for exactly two seconds before his face returns to its casual frown status. "Oh. Um. My last name is Barber. Ben Barber. Happy to help with your beautification project."

"Well...thanks for telling me about the...program, Ben Barber."

He nods. "Thank you for keeping our city clean."

4

BEN

"Beautification project." I groan for the fifteenth time as I drive home in the afternoon rush. I cannot believe I was this much of an idiot talking to Eila. Beautification project. I saw her flinch at those words and I just knew I messed up and said something weird.

What are the chances that I'd run into Eila again and then feel so surprised and excited that I just blurted the first dumb thing that came into my head?

I actually can believe I said that, because I always say the wrong thing. Should I have told her I'm autistic? I haven't told anyone yet.

I move through my day, thinking an inspection will drown out the voices in my head reminding me that I don't know how to talk to women—or anyone else for that matter. But instead, I just kept hearing myself say the same thing over and over and catching the squint in Eila's eye as she backed away.

I don't know why I'm harping on this. Eila Storm might like beer, but is she really going to be different from everyone else in my life? Everyone is always in on the same joke I can't seem to understand.

It's probably best if I focus on learning more about my neurodivergence right now, anyway. It turns out there is a lot to unpack. Dr. Morgan suggested a podcast where the autistic host interviews other autistic adults about their experiences, and I've been binging the entire backlist. It turns out there are terms for a lot of the aspects of my life that my mom always just called "Ben's weird little habits."

I'm not upset that I never got evaluated sooner. A lot of the studies and supports Dr. Morgan talks about weren't very common until I was in middle school anyway. It's been a real shock to my system realizing there's a new perspective I could take to my entire life, though. Like ... maybe I'm not a grumpy hermit. Maybe I just need to be alone after work to calm down after the exhausting challenge of trying to read other people for eight hours straight.

I walk up the steps to my house and I hear Maurice clicking down the hall as I fish out my keys.

"Hey, buddy, I'm here. Hang on." He yips, his unsteady gait creating a weird rhythm as he crashes into the door. "Maurice, just give me one minute. I'm excited to see you, too." I fling the door open and crouch down as he leaps into my arms, licking my entire face.

I found Maurice wandering along Hamilton Avenue at the end of a work day. I was out there inspecting some affordable housing projects before the electricians arrived. I heard a whimpering sound in one of the townhouses. This little three-legged dog was huddled in there, covered in fleas and grime.

I dropped by the animal shelter to get him checked out, but they couldn't identify an owner. He's been living with me ever since.

He stops licking my face and backs up, barking in earnest. "Right. Do you need to go out?" I reach for his leash on the table inside the door. I never felt like I needed a table there before I needed a place to store poop bags and a special harness the vet said would help him on his walks.

Maurice and his accessories have changed a lot about how I live and function in my own space. I was surprised that I didn't hate the adjustment the way I do most changes. As I'm learning, routine and predictability are important to autistic people. There's something comforting about just knowing that, and honestly, Maurice adds more predictability to my life since he, too, seems to thrive on routine.

Maurice trots to the table and sniffs at the drawer containing his outdoor getup. "Here we go, bud." I smile as we head back outside. Maurice doesn't care if I say things weird. As long as I fill his food and water dish and let him sleep in my bed, he's content. Content for Maurice usually means half asleep and snoring.

We wander along Moon Way and I'm glad when we don't see many other families out walking their dogs. I've got a backup plan if we do run into someone, but I'm still relieved it's just me and my hound today. Maurice is always calm with me, but he seems to get as wary with small talk as I do and often growls or whines when people stop and bring up sports.

One thing I felt proud of when I first met Dr. Morgan was the prepared responses I have for specific small talk. She says this is called scripting, and it's a tool I didn't even know I was using. Someone asks me about the weather? I automatically respond, "It'll be different in an hour." But in my head, I always growl that it's Pittsburgh. The weather is almost always the same: gray.

There's nothing gray about Eila Storm, though. I wonder why she intrigues me so much. I can tell right away there's very little predictability where it comes to her. I should feel terrified of a woman like that, and maybe I am. But above all else, I find her fascinating. One of the more confusing aspects of other people is the way they communicate feelings and emotions. Eila's mood always seems obvious to me, at least in the few times I've been in her presence. I think my sister would say Eila gives me good vibes.

Maurice barks as if he can read my thoughts and gives a little tug, pulling me faster. He likes to poop in the field at the end of the alley. I like him to finish before youth baseball practice starts in the afternoons. I'm not in the mood to tell children why my dog only has three legs.

I think back to when I used to play ball here. Catching a ball with my friend Cash. He was one of the few people who never seemed to make me feel like an outsider. Cash had a kid not long after high school and didn't have much time to hang out after that, so I'm left with Maurice.

He sniffs around the outfield looking for an ideal spot to crap, and I stare down at the city. It's a unique view of Pittsburgh from up here, the tops of all the buildings just visible over the crest of Greenfield's hilltops.

A car full of women in sun visors begins to unload along the curb and I groan. Ever since the city added pickle ball courts up here, we've been getting all sorts of people with opinions. They glare at me while Maurice does his business, like I'm not going to pick it up or something. I frown right back at them, knowing they're going to put garbage in the recycling bins. If anyone would bother to read the handout, they'd know the city doesn't recycle plastic sports drink bottles.

I stoop to bag up Maurice's situation, wondering how those women sleep at night knowing they contaminate entire barrels full of perfectly good recycling. Maurice looks at me as if to say *they don't even think about it, Ben.*

"You're right." I knot the bag and toss it into the black can, which is clearly for garbage. "Let's go."

He waddles back home, I toss his gear into the drawer before hanging my own bag on the hook. I should make dinner, but I still feel antsy and flustered after running into Eila this morning, so I sit down at my piano to work out my butterflies.

That's what my mother used to say when I'd pace or tap my fingers on the table at home. "You've got butterflies living in your bones. That or a swarm of bees!"

I smile, imagining Eila's hair hiding a swarm of bees. Nobody would be able to tell with all the grass and twigs she evidently keeps in there. I start to play, an old Grainger arrangement sneaking through my fingers as Maurice curls up on my feet. I don't need to use the pedals for this one, so I let him enjoy the vibrations of the piano against his old body.

My mother never seemed to understand me much, but she did have the idea to get me piano lessons. Who knows what she bartered in order to afford them initially. I didn't need them for long.

It turns out, I can just play the piano—the way some people can instinctively understand what other people mean when they talk. I glance at the sheet music a few times, and the music comes out of my fingers effortlessly. I can't explain it any better than I know what Eila Storm thought about me helping her clean out the garbage from her next-door lot.

I play the Grainger melody until my stomach gurgles and then I pull out the piano cover, hiding the keys beneath the chipped blond wood. "Someday we'll get a really nice piano," I tell Maurice.

And then, maybe someday I'll be able to play it for someone other than my dog.

5

EILA

I have carpenter ants everywhere.
They're in my light sockets.

ELIZA

Gross

EVA

[vomit emoji] are they in my
room???

ESTHER

Koa called an exterminator. But
we need to clear out for a few
hours. Eden, can we do family
dinner at yours and Eila's place?

ME

Sure, descend upon our manor

EDEN

I don't think it's a manor. Not with
our staircase situation.

ESTHER

Tell the landlord to fix the fucking
steps. Do I need to make a call?

ME

Stand down, sarge. It's fine. It's
also too hot to cook. I'll grab salad
stuff.

EVA

I just bought a toaster oven! I'll
bake a cake.

ELIZA

Pass on the toaster cake. See you
in 20.

I sit by the tower fan, exhausted. I cleaned out that entire lot today by myself.

Knowing the city was sending a trash truck was a huge relief, I didn't have to haul anything after that first load. I just sort of rolled the garbage bags to the street and sure enough, the stinky pickup arrived. The dudes inside gave me a salute as they left me with my half-acre of well-lit, decimated soil.

I already asked Eliza to bring me a barrel of goat crap from her herd so I can get a real planting going. She didn't even ask questions.

I planted an experiment a few weeks ago with some spliced hops I got from my recon up at the farm. My little plot of vines is thriving, despite being planted among heaps of litter and old tires. I wave my fingers at the hops through the window, smiling at the tiny plants who grew out of a literal trash heap to form something amazing.

But enough admiring. It is time to get my ass in gear and make some room in this place if my sisters are all coming over. I quickly sweep through the living room, moving Eden's beekeeping books from the chairs and stacking up my own research on the end table, out of the reach of the oscillating fan.

I wish I'd paid more attention to biology and science when I was in school. Esther says my brain was focused on other shit...like not having actual parents to take care of me. That's always an unpleasant rabbit hole and I avoid dwelling on that part of my life. I also argue that our high school teachers were just talking about boring crap. If I'd had the chance to study hydroponics and soil nutrients, I would have spent way less time trying to vape in the old planetarium.

I begin washing the dishes, trying to remember when we all moved in with Esther. I was already in high school when she came into her windfall, as she calls it, and bought her own house. She immediately took in the four of us, and for the first time in our lives, we knew for certain we'd have electricity and food in the cupboards. Our mom never seemed to notice that we'd left.

I'm not entirely different from those hop vines I have out back. I grew up amidst the aftermath of our mother's bad choices and, as soon as I had someone looking after me, I became productive.

At least ... I *was* productive. I got twitchy at my job faster than usual. I'm not surprised I got fired, not really. But after a weekend I can admit that it stings. I came damn close to crying when my boss let me go, and I'm at least glad I didn't show him how much it hurt to lose that job.

I did enjoy working with plants all day, tweaking soil and fertilizer. Sure, the customers drove me batty, but it's not like I'll ever be somewhere totally free from the public. I have to learn to keep my cool or I'm never going to keep a job.

I bite my lip. I was supposed to fill out the unemployment paperwork today. I got carried away with cleaning out the lot and then tidying up the house and, well, now it's past business hours.

Satisfied with my whirlwind house cleaning efforts, I make my way up to the bathroom for a shower, smiling in the natural light from the high windows. We rent an old house, and we've got a claw-foot tub that's been retrofitted for a shower. But the whole back wall has recessed shelves, where I imagine the homeowners from the 1900s stashed their gas lamps or whatever.

Me? I keep my plants there and I shower with them.

They thrive in the humidity. This room is bursting with leafy green goodness, and it gets ample sunlight.

I have just enough time to douse all the plants and scrub myself before I hear my sisters descend upon the house from downstairs.

I head down in my robe with a towel on my head, forgetting that Esther's married and there's a man among us now. My brother-in-law looks like he swallowed a fish bone. "Shit. Sorry, Koa. I'll throw on some clothes."

"No bother," he mumbles, staring down at his toes. Esther rolls her eyes and gestures for me to head up to my room.

I throw the towel in the hamper and yank on my cleanest pair of overalls with a tank. Modest enough for salad and toaster cake.

When I get back downstairs, Esther has my sisters set up in an assembly line, chopping and dicing stuff for the salad while Koa shreds a rotisserie chicken. Esther throws me a block of cheese. "Shred that. We'll sprinkle it on top."

I frown at the setup, which is a little uninspired. "I'll be right back in. I'm going to grab some herbs from outside."

Eliza points toward the window. "Oh, hey, I left you those buckets of crap you asked for." She laughs at her own joke. I give her a thumbs up and make my way down the rickety steps toward the little herb patch I put near Eden's hives.

"This is going to make a difference," I tell the room as I pop back inside with basil and mint. "And we don't need shredded cheddar on the salad. That's weird and it'll feel like school lunch in your mouth."

"But I like cheese." Eva pouts as she tries slicing cherry tomatoes with a dull-ass knife.

"Put cheese on your nachos for snack later, then."

"You've got a lot of opinions today, Eila. What's up?" Esther's entering her mom-mode and I don't hate it. I'm mature enough now to recognize how much Esther gave up to take care of us, how much she loves us and wants us to do well. But I do sometimes wonder what it would be like to just have a regular big sister instead of a pseudo-parent.

"I cleared out the vacant lot finally." I point out the window. "Like, cleared it. And I found out if you're cleaning up a vacant lot, the city will come haul away all the trash on it."

"Oh yeah?" Esther finishes slicing the cucumbers and moves on to opening a bag of croutons.

Eva clears her throat and wags her eyebrows at me. "Don't you have something else to share with our big sister?"

Eliza makes the hand gesture for "give me some money" and I glare at them both. Esther arches a brow and waits, expectantly, for me to spill.

"So, I lost my job on Friday." Esther opens her mouth to talk but I shake my head. "It's going to be okay. I'll go around tomorrow and file for unemployment and all that. Meanwhile, I have big plans for that space over there." The room is silent, so I continue. "I'm growing hops. You know, lean in on that 'buy local' energy. I'm going to sell to some of the local breweries. I can already tell my spliced bines will dig the extra space and sunlight."

The kitchen falls silent as we all wait to see if Esther will dole out sympathy or instructions or something else. Nervous, I keep rambling. "It's kind of late in the growing season, but I'm on top of it. I transplanted the hops from the farm, so it's not like I'm starting from scratch ..." Esther shakes croutons onto the giant salad and smiles at me empathetically. "Let me know when your beers are ready. I'll buy a keg for the bar."

My shoulders relax and I smile at her.

Declaring the salad good enough, Eden pulls out a vinaigrette that's mostly honey, and we all tuck in, jockeying for space where the oscillating fan at least puffs at us as it moves. I should be content with this, family dinner in the heat with the people I love most. With people I know have my back.

But I can't help feeling a yearn for more, for control over my own work, and for that work to feel meaningful. Eventually, Eva tries to serve her toaster cake and admits that it's a little spongey in the middle. Eden slathers it with honey and we all manage to eat a slice, toasting the effort.

Nobody mentions that Storm sisters can't bear to throw food away, not when we spent so much time without any. Nobody speaks aloud that we will always choke down half-raw food, burnt food, bland food because calories are calories and we all remember the grip of an empty tummy.

Esther divvies out the leftovers equitably, counting out individual lettuce leaves into sandwich baggies as Koa stares at the ceiling shaking his head. I pat my big sister on the arm and help her divide the remaining croutons until we have six tiny side salads and a chicken carcass. I say goodnight to my sisters, promising to boil the bones and make broth.

6

EILA

I MANAGE to snag a ride to the Shadyside neighborhood when Eden leaves to run errands in the morning. I need to collect my final paycheck, then head to the library for help getting unemployment set up.

Eden drops me off well before the nursery manager gets in for the day. But there are plenty of errands in the neighborhood I can catch up on while I'm not sitting on the bus waiting for every passenger to shuffle slowly down the aisle. I should look into one of those e-bikes.

As I debate the pros and cons of an e-bike compared to a car, I see a familiar figure squinting up at the sign for the pet store. I cup my hands over my mouth and shout, "Ben!" He doesn't turn. Odd.

I walk over to him from the coffee shop entrance, iced latte in hand, and tap him on the shoulder with my cold drink. He twitches and turns to face me, but he doesn't smile. "Oh," he stammers. "Oh. Hi."

I look at my watch. "They should be open. You going in?"

He sighs and shivers, despite the heat. "I just... hate it in there. I usually order dog food online and have it shipped but I ran out and forgot to adjust my subscription and Maurice is on special food I can't get at my preferred grocery store so—"

"Hey!" I place a hand back on his shoulder. "Slow down there, big guy. I hear you saying you don't like the vibe of Pet Mart?" He shakes his head rapidly. "Makes sense because it smells weird in there and the lights are always blinky."

Ben's face sags in apparent relief. "Yes. It's the lights. God, the lights. It just ... it makes my teeth hurt if that makes sense? I hate it so much."

I take a sip of my drink, noting that Ben studies my face as I do so. He seems to be easing out of his fluorescent-light-induced stupor. I tell him, "If you're willing to walk a few blocks, there's a great independent pet store near the nursery where I work...where I used to work."

He furrows his brows and scratches the back of his neck. "What makes it great?"

I take yet another sip of my drink, slurping up

the last bit of liquid around the ice cubes in my jar. Eden says it's obnoxious to walk around with glass jars and my own straw for my coffee, but she also rejects a ton of the glass jars my sisters give her to put honey in and I feel like it's better to use them than fill a landfill with coffee cups.

"Well," I rattle my ice cubes. "For starters, the owner is a kick-ass woman, which already makes it a highly functional business. She also does a lot of work with local rescues. And she sells cute sweaters and shirts for pets." I pause a moment and stare at him. "Does your pet have a capsule wardrobe? Because he could."

"Capsule wardrobe?" Ben looks dazed and I give his arm a gentle push to steer him toward Petagogy.

"Come on," I tell him. "I'll explain along the way." He walks beside me silently as I list all the raincoats and bandanas I've seen in the window of the shop. When we reach the cozy store on Ellsworth Avenue, Ben barely hesitates on the threshold as I push my way inside. "Hey, Heather!" I wave at the owner, who pops her head out from behind a mountain of dog food bags she's restocking.

"Oh, hey, Eila. Did you finally convince your sister to get a cat?"

I shake my head. "Nah. Still dreaming. My friend here needs some food for his..." I turn to face

Ben, who seems to be doing deep breathing exercises. "What kind of dog do you have, anyway?"

He clears his throat, his body visibly relaxes. "I think he's a terrier mix. Maybe some pointer in there. He's a rescue."

Heather nods and gestures around the store. "Well, let me know if you need any help. If there's something specific you need I can probably order it."

"We need a capsule wardrobe for Ben's pooch," I joke, and Heather laughs. I point at the rack of life vests. "We should start with sporting goods."

Ben looks at me, sternly. "Maurice has three legs and he's at least 12. I don't take him sporting." He holds up his fingers to form air quotes.

"Easy there. I'm just joking around. But really? Three legs?".

"Aw, a tri-paw'd." Heather clasps her hands in front of her heart. "You should bring him in sometime. I'd love to meet him."

Ben looks like someone just offered him a trip to Disney World, pulling out his phone as Heather asks him for pics of his dog. I glance over his shoulder and stare at the screen, seeing a wiry, cloudy-eyed dog curled up on a tuffet. Eventually, Heather gets back to her inventory, and Ben starts scanning the shelves for the special food.

"Wow, she's just got it right here." He holds up a small bag of kibble. I squint to read the label.

"Does that say ancestral grains? And pomegranate?"

Ben nods, grabbing a few more bags and holding them under each arm like footballs. "Maurice has had a hard life. He needs a balanced diet."

"You sound like a commercial." I read a bit more of the label. "I want to meet this dog, who eats trout and sweet potato with spelt and blueberry."

Ben looks at me, deadly serious. "You can meet Maurice any time you want, Eila."

It's my turn to shiver a bit, but I tell myself it's because of the air conditioning in Heather's store and not the intensity of Ben's gaze. "Well." I swallow and tuck my hair behind my ears. "I have to take care of some things." I gesture toward the nursery with my thumb. "You all set here? I guess I didn't think about you having to carry the heavy food to your car..."

"I'm great. Thank you, Eila, for showing me this place." He clears his throat and shifts his weight to better balance the dog food bags. "Maurice will be really happy, and I didn't have to deal with the atmosphere at Pet Mart..."

"Nobody wants to deal with Pet Mart, Ben."

He smiles. Just one side of his mouth hooks up, but his eyes light up with the gesture. He should look ridiculous, in his polo shirt with dog food bags under each arm. But with that smile and his shaggy hair and a jawline that could slice herbs...Ben Barber doesn't look ridiculous at all.

"Okay, well, see you around." I back out of the store and toss my remaining ice cubes into my mouth, crunching them between my teeth as I speed walk toward the nursery. This morning did not go as expected.

7

____

BEN

I'M NOT STALKING. It's not creepy if I swing by the intersection Eila mentioned last Monday ... I'd just be making sure the city sent a trash truck in response to the form I filed on her behalf. Not that there's really anything I can do if they didn't send a trash truck ... I don't have that kind of clout. Plus, it's been a week now.

She's just so ... overflowing each time I see her. It's like energy and confidence and spunk is all simmering inside her, a minute from bursting out. On Tuesday she had her nails painted and it changed the look of her hands. Still hard-working hands but tipped with sparkles. For the first time, I could imagine her hands both crushing a beer can *and* stroking Maurice.

I take a breath, realizing that I'm imagining Eila

meeting my dog. I can see it all so clearly: her kneeling on the floor and skritching his ears. Him licking her face. Her laughing about it. Is this what people are doing when they read fiction—imagining scenarios just like this?

I don't have the head space to think about how other people's brains work. I spent this entire week trying to figure out how my own brain works, reading things my therapist sent me about sensory overload and masking. We both agreed I've never done much work to mask the ways my autism impacts my interactions with others. Instead, I just spent a long time feeling like a weirdo.

Even though I know men often buy flowers for people they want to woo, I decide it would be crossing a line to stop and buy Eila flowers and based on our conversation from the bar that first night, I'd be worried I'd get the wrong type and upset her. Or insult her by patronizing the business that fired her.

No, I'm just going to drive over to her house, look around, and hope like hell she's home. Which is a terrible idea, because this is absolutely not the right time for me to get involved with someone romantically. Not that she's at all interested in that way with me, or so I think. And yet, I time things so I'm in the Garfield neighborhood on an inspection for my last stop of the day, figuring an unemployed person might just be home when I swing by.

The street is void of cars when I arrive, but Eila Storm is a car-free person.

I can tell I'm in the right place because the only occupied house on the block simply has to belong to her. The wood siding has seen its better days, but it's painted a bright teal. Every inch of the porch is covered in plants, leaves curling toward the after-noon sun, bright orange blooms beckoning me from the street. The humid heat seems to lessen its hold on the air near Eila's house, like I can feel all her flowers exhaling and it creates a fragrant breeze. The air smells sweet and pungent, like honeysuckle.

I see bee boxes in the side yard, and I frown, feeling my work-brain kick into gear.

Does Eila have the right paperwork filed for those? I try not to focus on other violations. There's no handrail on the steps...she's probably renting but sending her landlord a citation could activate a wa-terfall of problems. "I'm just here to check on the garbage in the lot next door," I mutter to myself. I close my eyes and approach the property, peering up at the vacant area, wondering if Eila is nearby... wearing overalls.

I can tell Eila did a lot of work up here. She seems to have indeed sawed each of the tires in half to form a boundary fence. It also looks like she raked the flat areas. No trash bags in sight. No Eila in sight either...

I shield my eyes from the sun and look around, deciding I'll count to sixty before I leave. Surely, I can get away with one solid minute of gazing without seeming like a threat to whomever might see me out here.

As I stare at the lot, trying not to look like a serial killer, I grow uncomfortable. Eila didn't just clean up the space. She's got something going on over here...something unpermitted. Something off book. I swallow. It's one thing to turn a blind eye to the sins of her landlord, but quite another for me to know she's cultivating city-owned property.

I close my eyes and try to breathe deeply. I feel myself spiraling. We don't know it's city owned. We don't know if the actual owner is decades behind on any taxes. We don't know. We don't know...

"Ben Barber? Is that you?"

I open my eyes to find Eila stomping toward me in muck boots and, of course, overalls. She's clearly been at work in the soil for hours today. Her arms are streaked with dirt and her tanned skin glistens a bit with sweat. She's dewy. That's a fun word to say and I like how it feels in my mouth. I never thought about what that word meant before now, but Eila Storm glistens with dew. She is remarkable. I clear my throat. "Hi. I...uh...well I wanted to see if the trash guys ever came. I mean the waste management team." I flap a hand behind me hoping she fills in the gaps.

She grins. "They came right away! Thank you for that. I've gotten so much done. Doesn't it all look great?"

I squeeze my eyes shut, not wanting to be forced to look at her illegal activity, knowing I'll have no choice but to act. Closing my eyes helps me filter out all the noise—internal and external—and focus on what I need to do next. Deep breath, I also know that squeezing my eyes shut in front of people makes them uncomfortable. I've learned that. So, I open them again as Eila begins speaking.

"There's no water on this side, obviously, but Eden and I have enough barrels set up that we have plenty of agua to spare. Gotta love that Pittsburgh rain, am I right?"

"The rain really gets in the way of my work, actually. But I know yours benefits from wet weather."

She nods. "My sisters were skeptical, but things have already started growing. Benny boy, I know this is going to be amazing."

I take a deep breath. "You know...so, actually... god." My skin is crawling and I'm sweating. I have to act. Fuck it. "Eila, you can't just grow things on city property."

She presses her lips together and frowns at me. Her eyes harden. "What do you mean?"

I wave at the vacant lot. "You told me you were cleaning up the garbage. That's generous and we appreciate that."

"We?"

I nod. "We. Like the city employees. My colleagues."

Eila crosses her arms over her chest. "You told me you were a construction inspector. What are you going to do? Rip up my plants?"

I shake my head. "Eila. You're trespassing." I wring my hands together, squeezing my fingers until the tips turn white. She looks confused and angry. So angry. I should tell her I'm autistic.

She charges on, yelling. "I don't understand what's happening here. First you stare at me while I'm out drinking with my sisters, then you buy me a drink and act all chummy and smitten. Then you pretend to help me so you can, what? Trap me into expensive citations I can't afford? I honestly thought we were becoming friends. I'm just here trying to improve the fucking soil and prevent erosion on neglected property."

"You're not wrong, Eila. It's just that there are protocols. Procedures." *Did she say friends? God, I've ruined everything, including my attempts to woo her.*

She snorts. "How long does that all take? Real quick, I'm sure."

With great reluctance and a sinking heart, I pull my notepad from my back pocket. I'm still wearing my uniform. I'm still City Employee Ben, not Regular Guy Ben. I almost laugh at the thought of myself as regular. Nobody has ever described me that way. Autistic Ben doesn't understand people and has to follow the rules, or he has panic attacks. Autistic Ben is perfect for inspection work but shit at human interactions. "I have to shut this down, Eila. Whatever it is, it breaks the rules."

Her nostrils flare as I fill out the citation on my note pad. My stomach churns and I start sweating, knowing I'm ruining any potential for anything with this fascinating woman but I'm incapable of not proceeding.

I feel a lump growing in my throat. I struggle to swallow. I hand her the paper, she refuses to accept it in her hand.

"I'd ask you to leave, but this is city property and I'm not in charge." She sniffs and backs up toward what I hope is her own yard, where I also hope she has permission to keep those damn bees.

The pink citation flutters in the breeze before it lands in the dirt near my feet. Do I cite her for littering as well? Or is this one my fault because I released the piece of paper? Why the hell am I like this?

I stoop to pick up the pink ticket and, seeing no sign of Eila, I set it gingerly in her mailbox as I make my way back to my car. Along the way, I panic at the thought that it might be illegal to put something inside someone's mailbox. I sprint back up the steps, grab the pink ticket, and feel my heart begin to race.

8

BEN

WHAT DO I DO? What do I do? What the hell do I do?

My skin is buzzing and crawling, and I rock side to side in the seat of my car. When I was younger, I used to rock and shake all the time and it drove my family bananas. It's been a long time since I felt this upset, frustrated, overwhelmed.

I think about calling my therapist, but what could she do to help? Dr. Morgan can't take back my actions. She can't reverse time.

I can't let go of the vision of Eila's eyes, stone cold and unforgiving. I don't know where to go or whether I should even process the paperwork on my end. Who can I talk to? Who would tell me the right thing to do?

I sit twitching in my official City of Pittsburgh electric vehicle, trying to think. I cannot confide in a colleague right now. Some of them are clearly very skilled in talking to women but would very likely skip over my discomfort and chastise me for getting behind on my inspection schedule.

I let out a humming sound as I drive toward my mother's house. I promised I'd take a look at her ceiling after work today and I don't know how to explain why I'm too upset to do it. I park outside her house and tap on the door as I enter the living room. "Mom? It's Ben."

"Hey, Benny." Mom rushes toward me from the kitchen and I brace myself. As per usual, she plants a too-soft touch on my cheek and kisses me with a loud "mwah" sound. I know I shouldn't flinch at my mother's touch. I know it upsets her. Today it all feels worse than normal, perhaps because I'm already squirming over what I did with Eila.

"Show me the ceiling," I tell her, trying to keep my voice pleasant. I know my face looks strange when I force a smile, but I also know my mother likes me to appear happy. I guess I do mask my autism, sometimes. I catch the hurt in her eyes as Mom nods and walks toward the dining room.

"The landlord sent someone to paint, but it just looks worse than before." She points at a large wet spot above the dining table.

I frown. "That's water damage, Mom. You can't

paint over it. Did they find the source of the problem?"

She holds her hands up. "How should I know? I called about the weird spot. They sent a painter while I was at work."

I consider my growing list of follow-up questions, trying to prioritize them so my mother won't think I'm being stubborn and relentless. "Would you like me to call the landlord for you?" I lick my lips, not sure if I hope she says yes.

"Lord no, Benny. I can't have you chewing him out. Next thing he'll raise the rent again. Just tell me what to say and I'll figure out how to say it nicely."

I close my eyes. The landlord should send a plumber to address the obvious water leak. Why is this complicated? I don't think I was meant to navigate the human world, with so many nuances and non-universal rules. Gray areas make me sweat.

I wish I could just summarize all this on a piece of paper, and then ask my mom for advice about the Eila situation. But I can't figure out a way to do any of that without first telling my mom about my diagnoses. I haven't prepared for that conversation at all.

No, I exhaust my family just trying to exist in a society where people say they're going to get "a couple things," and come out of the store with more than two items.

I make a list for my mom, sticking as close as I

can to nouns and verbs only. She pats my hand, which feels a lot better than my face and I turn the ends of my mouth up in a small smile. Mom asks, "Did you eat? Do you want to stay for dinner?"

I shake my head and look out the front window at the Greenfield neighborhood where I've lived my entire life never quite fitting in. And then I remember there is someone in my life who sees nothing wrong with my rigid approach to the rules at work. Cash Brennan once called me to tip me off about a heap of code violations in his now-girlfriend's commercial gym.

I know Cash knows about women, because his girlfriend lives with him, despite his efforts to uproot her business initiatives.

He texts me sometimes. I occasionally see him out working on projects. I can contact him. It's better than boiling over in panicked frenzy alone.

I pat Mom's hand with my other one and explain, "I'm meeting a friend, actually. I gotta go."

Mom's face brightens at the word friend as she hustles me out the door, promising to follow up with the landlord soon. I try not to think about the ceiling falling in before she gets around to making the call. I have more pressing worries right now...

I know it's considered rude to show up to visit someone unannounced, but driving to Cash's house is faster than pulling over to text him and wait for his response.

Please let him be home.

I park near his house, adjust the collar on my polo shirt, and knock on the door. It opens and my eyes sink down to where Cash's young daughter stands, frowning. I know he has a child, but I always forget.

"Who are you?" She squints up at me but doesn't open the door all the way.

"Hi. I, uh, know your dad. Is he home?"

"He is." She doesn't move and I smile, realizing I've done what others are always doing to me, tripping me up in social situations. I didn't ask her the correct question, the one that would tell me what I want to know. I asked her the question society suggests should come first. I sort of like that she responded this way.

"Sorry. I meant to say, would you tell him Ben Barber is here to see him?"

The kid squints at me and shuts the door. I hear her running off through the house and, thirty seconds later, I'm staring into the perplexed, bearded face of Cash Brennan. He swings the door open and gestures for me to come inside.

"Long time, no see, man. You want something to drink?" He looks over his shoulder, where his daughter is dancing in the living room. "I've got apple juice, water, and some sort of fermented tea that Piper likes. I think it tastes like piss, but your mileage may vary."

"My mileage?"

He shakes his head. "Never mind. Let me get you a water. Sit down."

I pull out a chair in the dining room, noticing that the walls of Cash's house are covered in kid drawings and family photographs. A lot of them look candid. My mom always tried to get me and my sister in matching outfits in the studio at JCPenney. Then the bright lights would pound down on me, and the photographer would say weird, confusing things to coax me to smile and it wouldn't work. I always winced. And later, my mother would look at the pictures and cry.

I glance at Cash, approaching with a glass of water and his signature scowl. Some people just have frowning faces. "Thank you." I reach for the glass and take a hesitant sip. I can always taste it if someone is using ice from an ice maker in their freezer. It just tastes...salty or something. I hate it.

But Cash's cubes appear homemade, from a tray. The water is flavorless and perfect. I gulp some down and he slides a coaster toward me. I arch a brow, impressed.

"Sooo..." he pauses, looks at me and sighs.

"What's up, dude? You don't usually drop by like this."

I nod and drag a hand down my cheek. My stubble is coming in. I'll need to shave again when I get home. Some days it seems to grow faster than others. Or I'm just more aware of it. "I need advice."

Just then the back door opens, and Piper sings her way into the kitchen. "Hello, family! Is everyone ready to smell like garlic? 'Cause I'm making falafel and—oh. Ben?"

My mouth works up and down as the words leave me. Cash gestures at me with his water glass. "Ben needs advice. He was about to explain."

Cash's daughter runs through the room and crashes into Piper, who scoops her up in a jiggly hug before plunking her back on the ground. I'm always surprised when people enjoy that kind of thing. I hated hugs as a kid. But maybe I just hated when adults gave them to me with no advanced notice. Ruby—that's her name!—seemed to expect that embrace and looked forward to it.

"Sorry, Ben. Go on." Piper sits in the chair next to Cash and drapes her body over his side. It looks uncomfortable. Neither of them seems to think so. I clear my throat.

"I met the one."

They stare, unblinking.

"A woman. She's the one for me. End game."

Cash's eyes widen and his red brows disappear up under his hair. "That's great, Ben. What's your move? How can we help?"

I describe seeing her at the bar, my fascination with her hair, the way she insisted I buy her a beer. How I sent the city trash truck to help her haul garbage from the lot next door.

"She sounds fascinating," Piper says, shifting in her seat to lean her chin on her elbows on the table. Cash wraps a hairy arm around her back, his palm rubbing slow circles, like he's not even conscious of doing so. "What happened next?"

I roll my lips inside my mouth and bite down on them, a bad habit I thought I'd broken. I release them with a click. "I wrote her a citation for trespassing on the vacant lot next to her house."

Cash groans. Piper's arms slowly sink to the table and her jaw slackens. "I know. I know. That's why I'm here. I still have the citation." I pull it from the pocket of my polo shirt. "I haven't filed it yet. But I have to. I'm a city inspector and she's breaking all kinds of rules."

Cash squints at me as I list her transgressions. "I crushed her dreams instead of wooing her and now she hates me. And I'd like to fix it if it's at all possible."

He sits back in his chair, crossing his arms over his chest. "I know this is going to sound hypocritical of me, since I actually sent you on purpose to shut down Piper's business." And it's true that he did that. He called me and told me about her operating a business in a property that was horrifically unsafe, and I had no choice but to act.

Piper punches Cash in the arm and he doesn't react. "I just need you to know, Ben, that this is not a great strategy to win over *the one*." He pulls out his fingers to make air quotes and I wish I hadn't said that about Eila.

It's statistically improbable that each person should have a designated, predetermined soul mate. The chances that I'd find mine in the same city seem so outlandish. And yet...Eila captivates me. "Well, what do I do? Do either of you have advice?"

Piper leans forward and snatches the citation from my fingers and starts ripping it up. My heart races and I lean forward to grab the pieces, but Cash sweeps them off the table and onto the floor. Piper points a finger at me. "First, you are not citing her for trespassing. It's bad enough you shut down her garden without talking to her more about it. Tell me and Cash the main problems with her *trespassing*. There has to be a way she can plant stuff there if that's what makes her happy."

"Of course there's a way. There's a whole process she didn't follow, paperwork she didn't fill out, permits she didn't apply for..."

I drift off as Cash and Piper stare at one another and shake their heads. I think I see Cash roll his eyes. "Pipes, do we have ink in the printer?" She nods and Cash turns to face me, sighing. "Ben, come with me to my office."

9

EILA

My sister Eden takes one look at me and declares an emergency Storm session. She calls Esther rather than text; in case our oldest sibling is already at work at the bar. "This looks like a hurricane about to happen," Eden whispers into the phone, as if I'm not standing a foot away from her growling and banging my fist on the counter. "Can you come over?"

Eva and Eliza are nearby finishing up work for the day and Eliza offers to give Eden a ride, since even my sister's goat van is faster than the city bus Eva normally depends on.

Eden points at me. "Go take a shower. You've got mulch in your eyebrows. By the time you get down here, everyone will be here, and you can spew it all out."

I growl in response and stomp upstairs, kicking off my overalls and climbing in the shower immediately. The cold water shocks me out of the worst of my rage cloud. What the hell kind of weirdo stares at me, acts like he's infatuated, and then stops by unannounced to cite me for trespassing on the lot he helped me de-garbage?

I slap a washcloth around my body for a bit and quickly shampoo my hair before leaving in conditioner in an attempt to tame my waves. It won't work in this humidity, but it's worth trying. And then I sigh and water the plants, thankful that I keep them in the shower and glad they always seem to ground me.

By the time I head downstairs in a fresh t-shirt and a pair of sturdy shorts, my sisters are all passing out takeout containers in Eden's and my cramped kitchen. I inhale, catching a whiff of curry. "Oh, thank god, one of you brought Indian food."

"That was Koa's idea," Esther says, referring to her husband. "He predicted a spicy mood and suggested matching food."

"This is why we like him," Eva says, beaming. She still lives with Esther and Koa, which makes sense because she's the youngest and barely an adult. Our crap mom blew town completely a few years ago to take a job as a card dealer in a cruise ship casino, but Eva was already living with Esther.

We're better off without Mom asking us for money for smokes.

I sink into a stool, irritated with our mother now as well as Stranger Ben.

Esther hands me a plate of rice with a few different dishes spooned on top. It smells amazing and I take a huge bite before muttering my thanks through a full mouth. She waits until I swallow and then says, "Now spill. I've got Tilly running the bar alone during happy hour."

I groan and slump back against the wall, balancing the plate on my legs. "It really was the perfect idea."

"Oh, god, here we go." Eliza reaches for a piece of naan to keep herself quiet as I glare at her.

"I mean it. I have all this extra time now, without a day job. And you know I've been researching hops. I seriously know a ton about how they grow." My sisters chew their food quietly, waiting for me to get to the part that sent me into a Storm rage, as Eden calls it when I freak out.

"We have like a zillion vacant lots in this city! One is right next door along half of the rest of this block. Right now, it's a hot mess, with people just dumping trash and tires in there or kids climbing the fence to sit in there and smoke."

"Because you never did that." Esther sets her

empty plate on the table and dusts off her hands before crossing her arms.

"The point is... the hops will grow on these lots. They're hearty, they climb, and with a little work I can even keep the knotweed at bay." I turn to face Eliza. "No worries, sis. There will always be enough invasive plants for your goat crew to eat." She holds her hands up to indicate she's not concerned about her own business. I sigh again, with less conviction. "I planted a few rhizomes next door just to see, and it worked perfectly. Perfectly! I can have a profitable crop in three years and then one lucky local brewery can brag about total local microeconomy with their beer. It was all going to plan."

"Until?" Esther arches a brow at me.

"Until the stupid man-bear-pig I met at that dive bar ruined everything."

"Oh, he was cute!" Eden turns to Eva and explains how the dark-haired, frowny faced man stared at me in wonder until I went over there and apparently talked with him for an hour. "What did he do to ruin your farm dreams?"

I pull Ben's business card from under my sunglasses on the edge of the counter and wave it around. Esther snatches it from my hands. "Ben Barber? Oh, I know that asshole. He's the one who shut down Piper's first gym space." She snorts. "He also tried to issue me a citation once. I did not go easy on him."

Eliza pats her shoulder. "Wouldn't expect you to, sis."

Esther rips up the card. "He's not going to follow up with this. Nobody in city government has time to care about you trespassing by way of attempting to beautify a vacant lot. He can't prove you planted a food crop there with intent to sell it, without a permit."

"Of course he can't prove it."

Esther squints at me. "Because you don't have a damn permit, Eila. You can't sell food without paperwork. It's not like flowers." Eden wriggles uncomfortably on her own stool and I keep quiet about her budding empire selling the honey she's been collecting from her various bee hives.

The sting of tears threatens to crack through my armor, and I know I shouldn't need armor with my sisters but I can't help it. I can't handle this idea falling apart and I really can't handle hearing how Esther really feels about my project.

"You sold some of my home brews at Bridges and Bitters last year," I retort.

Esther closes her eyes and swallows. "Trust me when I tell you that, ever since the fire, I've paid a lot more attention to the rules and regulations. I'm not even using second-hand candles at Bridges and Bitters anymore. Everything is totally above board. Not even Ben Barber could find something to cite in my establishment."

I snort. "I bet you twenty bucks he could."

"Much as I'd love to take you up on that wager, I have to get to the bar and relieve Tilly." Esther squeezes my shoulder as she walks toward the kitchen door. "I'm not saying your idea is bad, sissy. I'm saying you skipped over a big portion of the planning for it."

"And I told you I spent the entire day researching. I'm all in on this idea, Esther. It has legs, I tell you."

Esther closes her eyes and takes a deep breath, but before she can talk, Eden says in a quiet voice, "I thought you were getting with unemployment today?"

My cheeks heat. I was supposed to do that. And I know Eden is worried about the rent, and rationally I know that's a reasonable concern. I snap at her anyway. "Well, I didn't get around to it yet. Like I said I was busy with my new business."

Esther silently leaves the kitchen to go back to work, shaking her head. Eden glares at me and stomps upstairs. I finish the rest of my curry in silence, staring at the rest of my sisters until they start talking about Eliza's plan for her goats this coming winter.

10

———

EILA

"THERE'S A MAN ON THE PORCH!" Eden shouts into my bedroom before my alarm buzzes. I passed out in my stretchy shorts after stuffing my face with Indian food and I'm slow to sit up and rub the sleep from my eyes.

"What?"

Eden tugs her robe tighter across her body. She wakes up early like me, but doesn't usually start her workday until mid-morning. "The man from the bar, who ruined your life, is on our porch. With papers."

"Fuck." I fling out of the bed and shove my feet into a pair of flip-flops, clacking down the steps without stopping to pee. "What could he want?" I shout this over my shoulder before opening the door and snarling, "What do you want?"

He shouldn't look this good, leaning on a pillar with one arm above his head, his damn polo shirt clinging to muscles I never noticed before now. Before I hated him.

Ben startles and takes a step toward me, glancing up and down my body before directing his eyes to the folder in his hand. "I was hoping I could speak with you."

"About what? More shit you want to fine me for?" I fold my arms over my chest and lean against the door frame.

He shakes his head. "No. The opposite. I want to help you."

"I don't need your help, fuck you very much."

My sister shouts from upstairs. "Do you want me to call Koa to come over?"

"No. I'm fine. I've got the bat right here if I need it." Eden and I have a bunch of softball bats around the house, not because we think we need protection, but because she organized a rec league one time and forgot to return the equipment.

Ben peers around my shoulder to the row of metal bats propped against the wall by the stairs and rocks back on his heels.

He drags a hand through his hair. "I messed up. I was hoping I could try again."

"Try again to what?" I squint at him and look for signs of that triplicate notebook he pulled out of nowhere to write me a ticket. He's got on a pair of Dickies and a belt under that polo, and the combination, frankly, works for him. *God. Get it together, Eila Storm.* We hate him.

Ben clears his throat. "I'd like to woo you."

I shouldn't laugh, but the sound escapes my throat before I can control myself. "You what? Did you say woo?"

Eden appears over my shoulder, poking my collarbone with her chin. "He said woo," she echoes.

Ben blinks, looking uncomfortable. "I'd like to... make up for yesterday. And also see if you'll consider maybe going on a date...with me... Romantically."

Eden squeezes my hip. "Be gentle with him, Eila. Look how hard he's trying right now."

I roll my eyes so hard my stomach turns. "Why would I go out with someone who cited me for trespassing?"

"I ripped up the ticket, I swear!" He holds his empty palm up. "Can we sit? I brought something for you."

I squint at the folder but decide it can't hurt to look at it. "You've got five minutes. I have to finish applying for unemployment."

"I have to work, too. This will be quick. Honest."

I sit on the top step and he sinks down beside me, opening the folder. I see Adopt a Lot scrawled across a form with a lot of tiny print and a lot of boxes to fill in. Ben points a clean finger at the form. "I'd like to help you approach your beer project the right way—the formal way—and then see if I have any contacts in that department to help things move quickly for you. If we can fill this out soon, I can even have the lead test guy come out next week. He's joining me on another inspection nearby anyway."

I blink at the paper. It all looks very official and reads like a textbook. There's a reason I ran far, far away from anything involving a textbook, as fast as I could. I don't want to admit to him that the forms intimidate me; however, so I snatch the folder from him and pull it closer to my face.

I can feel him staring as I try to read the instructions. "Does this say lease? I already pay rent here," I tell him. "I'm not paying rent to improve a piece of land that's just sitting here rotting."

Ben leans back a bit and stares at me. "So...you want to plant things and sell them at a profit, on land you do not own? Like...a freeloader?"

"It's not like that." I point at the lot. "Erosion is a thing. Blight is a thing. I'd be doing the city a favor and fixing the soil, keeping it nice. Who knows? Maybe if this lot looks nice, someone will actually buy that house across from it." I hook a thumb at the vacant building that's a heartbeat away from getting condemned, probably sooner if Ben has anything to say about it.

He nods his head. "I hear you. And I think you're right, and that this lot adoption program would be great. I wanted to offer to help you with the process."

I look at the papers again. "It says I can't profit from anything I grow."

He looks again. "There's another section for what you have in mind. But there are FDA regulations. I can help. I'm great at this type of lingo."

"Confident much?" I scowl at the forms again, seeing numbers and code abbreviations and Roman numerals galore. I definitely need his help if I have any hope of going about this in an above-board manner. "This all seems way too complicated. I swear I can grow this shit and sell it all before I even manage to translate this application."

He shakes his head. "You can't sell it, though. Not to any reputable brewer. I have no doubt that you'd grow the most delicious hops in all the land. Let me help you make it official."

I fold my arms around the folder and stare at him. "What makes you so confident I can grow good hops?"

He stares at me again, intently. His eyes are brown, but in the morning sun with my blurry no-contacts vision, I can see little flecks of gold mixed in. "Because everything about you is amazing, Eila."

I'm not sure what to make of this comment, so I stand up, keeping the folder tucked against my side. I really need to pee now and I'm dying to put my contacts in so I can actually see the outlines of things. "Come back tomorrow after work and we'll talk."

He seems undeterred by my brevity and holds a hand to steady my elbow as I stumble on the top step leading up to the door. I yank my arm away from him and glower. Mostly because it shouldn't feel so arousing to have this man do something nice for me.

"Can I get your number? In case there's a problem?" He waits a beat and fishes a pen from the pocket of his polo shirt, waving it at me.

I sigh and scratch out my cell number quickly on the folder, half hoping he can't read my handwriting. I rip off the corner with my number and hand it to him, then stare in wonder as he slides it into his pocket, reverently patting it and grinning as he backs off my porch.

11

———————

BEN

I'M USUALLY VERY good at ignoring other things and focusing on my work. But today, knowing that I get to spend time with Eila Storm later, I'm distracted. I'm missing important things. Back at the office for a meeting, my attention is drawn to my co-worker Ulrich, who rolls a shiny metallic coil between his brown fingers the entire time our boss talks about zoning regulations and updates to building codes.

I normally enjoy updates to building codes. I find it soothing to pore over the details, to think about all the pieces that have to work in harmony for a building to function at its best. Not many people appreciate the importance of good duct-work, but I view it as the lungs of a building.

Except today. Today I can only stare at Ulrich's hands twirling that metal, thinking how close it is in color to the dark red of Eila's lips, how nicely it con-trasts to the dark curtain of her wild hair.

Ulrich snaps his fingers in my face, realizing I've been staring, the meeting is over, and we're the last ones in the room. "Sorry," I mutter, gathering my notepad. "Didn't mean to stare."

"Am I gonna have to catch you up later or did you catch any of that?"

I wave a hand. I can read the files online later. Not after work, obviously, because I'm going to Eila's house. But sometime soon. I watch as he slides the distraction back in his pocket. "What is that thing, anyway?"

"This?" He pulls it back out and holds it in his palm. "I think I took this from my kids last week. They were fighting over it. I think it's one of those fidgets."

"Fidgets?"

He nods and slips the coil onto his finger like a ring. I see that it's not rounded but, rather, spiked. "Kids today mess around with crap like this or those spinner things. It's supposed to help them focus on school or something." He holds it out between his thumb and forefinger, and I reach for it, stretching the pointy spring onto my own finger. "Now you're supposed to roll it up and down. I don't know, I thought it felt weird."

As I move the red fidget ring I nearly gasp. For as

long as I can remember, I've preferred this type of touch—rough, with a bit of a bite to it—rather than anything gentle. To me, a soft hand is like nails on a chalkboard to others. But this? "It's nice," I tell Ulrich.

"Hurts so good, eh?" He claps me on the back. "Keep it. My wife tells me she has an entire sack of them. Not sure why my kids thought it was worth beating each other to death over the red one." He walks out of the room, leaving me alone to marvel at the fidget ring. I start to wonder if I could wear ten of them, just jab right through the calloused skin on my hands to offer the perfect amount of stimulation.

I slide it into my pocket before I head to my next project, and I spend the rest of the day grabbing it whenever I feel my attention wander. It's like a small alarm clock or something. Marvelous.

After work, as I gather the printed forms Eila will need to fill out her applications properly, I slide the ring back on. I worry it up and down each finger incessantly as I drive toward her house, mount the inadequate stairs to her front door. Only when I raise my hand to knock, do I see the ring and think that it might be considered odd. I'm sticking it back in my pocket, wishing I had a loop or lanyard for it or something to prevent me losing it, when I hear Eila calling to me from the lot next door.

"Hey, Ben. I'm over here trespassing. You want to wait there or come help me finish watering?"

I adjust my collar and stare at her, lugging a hose from her own back yard to the rows of plants she's cultivated in what I'm certain is lead-filled soil. This negotiation with her is not going to be easy. I can't explain why I'm taking this on. What is it about the toned calves sticking out above her rain boots, leading up to trim thighs and cut-off jean shorts and...holy shit.

Eila wears a faded, cropped, ripped tank top that barely covers anything. She sprays the hose on the plants as if she is totally unaware that the water splashes back onto her chest. It's like a scene from the porn DVDs my high school classmates used to watch in their parents' basements. I never saw the appeal at the time, but now...

Now that there's a real woman in front of me shaking her hair in the sun, watering her illegal garden, half naked. I sink to the porch steps, not knowing what will happen if I approach her. Not even the fidget ring calms me down and I try to stare straight ahead while Eila works. She didn't invite me to ogle her. I'm here to try and win her over.

I remind myself she's not *just* the most attractive woman I've ever seen in real life. She's got an energy about her, a fierce tenacity, and a sense of confidence. I'm drawn to her, like a gnat to flypaper. I have to remember to be careful. I already told her how I feel. She has all the power right now.

Eventually, she winds up the hose and stalks toward me through the too-tall grass, a half-smile teasing her lips. She wipes her hands on her thighs, and I can see streaks of water running through the dirt all over her. She must not mind walking around filthy. Just the thought of feeling all that muck ordinarily makes me shiver, but there's something about seeing the dirt streaked on Eila that makes me want to scrub her clean with my bare hands. "Well, Benny, it's stinking hot inside. Where should we go to work on this?"

12

EILA

"WHEN DID THIS PLACE OPEN?" Ben looks around in wonder at the giant warehouse-turned-duckpin-bowling alley.

I shrug. "About a year ago. It's air conditioned. The bowling is cheap. My sisters and I come here a lot."

Ben jumps as someone behind us rolls a strike. The tiny wooden pins clatter to the lane before getting yanked up by the string attached to each one. He and I spread our stuff on a table near the bowling lanes, where I figure the serving team won't notice that we haven't booked a game or ordered any food.

I glance toward the swinging door to the back room where the brewers work on a schedule I haven't quite hammered down. "Sometimes I bend the owner's ear about his procurement. I get the sense he doesn't take me seriously, though." Not seeing anyone I know. I grab a few plastic cups from a stack at the end of the table.

Ben cocks a brow. "Perhaps because you drink their water and use their air conditioning without paying?"

I shake my head, laughing. "Touché." Free ice water from the carafe makes for the perfect punctuation mark on this ad hoc session. "Should we get started?"

Ben nods and points to some of the forms. "The first step is actually pretty easy. You just pick a category, name the plot of land, and file for your lead testing. I took the liberty of pulling the file for the lot next to your house. It's been vacant for decades."

I nod. "Sure has. I can't even find evidence of any more settling where the foundation was. I checked before I planted the hops. Because nobody cares about that land but me."

He clears his throat. "Until now."

"Are you here as my friend or Inspector Ben? Hm?"

He grunts and writes some things down on the form. "Is it really a set of paper forms? We don't fill it out online?"

Ben arches a brow at me. "Have you lived in Pittsburgh long? Of course it's a paper form."

We share a laugh and I look over his arm as he fills out the forms. "This doesn't seem too bad."

"It really isn't. At this stage. Here." He slides the paper across the table but jumps again as a group of bowlers shouts in excitement.

"Are you going to be okay here? We can go someplace else."

Ben looks a little sweaty, his eyes darting side to side like he's overwhelmed. A little like he looked outside that pet store he didn't want to go inside. I nod with understanding. "This is like the blinking lights for you, right? Too much?" I scoop up the papers and jerk my chin toward the door. "Let's go."

Ben trots behind me. "But you're hot, you said. I can be uncomfortable." Someone kicks the music into high volume and Ben shudders. I roll my eyes at the folly of it all.

"There are plenty of quiet places with air conditioning. Let's get you out of here." I place a hand on his shoulder and steer him outside, and as we step onto the sidewalk, I can feel him relax just as quickly as I feel the humid air surge around me. I groan. Ben sighs.

He starts to tug at his hair. "I wish I weren't like this. I wish I could just go to the stupid bowling alley."

I don't like how upset he seems about his reaction to all the noise in there. "I should have checked with you before we went inside. Not everyone likes loud noises."

Ben kicks at some gravel. "Normal people can sit inside a bowling alley without panicking."

I didn't realize it was bad enough that he felt panic. "Hey," I reach for his arm and steer him around the corner, walking toward a grassy parklet with a bench. "Come on. Normal people don't keep mental lists of places to mooch air conditioning, either, but you seem to tolerate me okay." Ben looks at me, like he's trying to decide if it's all right to believe me. "What's with the emphasis on being normal?"

He drags his hands through his hair again and drops into the bench, elbows on his knees, forehead in his hands. "All I ever hear, from everyone, always, is how abnormal I am. How difficult it is to know me because I make everything so hard."

I sit next to him. "You make everything hard? How so? Are you saying I'm not the first person you've gone all 'rigid inspector' around?" I nudge him with my shoulder, but I can tell he's not in the mood for jokes.

He stares at the traffic, and I revel in the slight breeze we get each time a car drives past. He clears his throat and says, "I recently found out I'm autistic."

"Oh." I'm not sure what to say beyond that, but I can tell that was a hard thing for him to disclose, so I say, "Want to talk about it?"

"I'm still figuring a lot of things out." He continues to stare ahead, and I smile, seeing some lightning bugs begin to pulse their yellow glow in the twilight. "But I guess that's why it's hard for me to be in the pet store. And the bowling alley. And basically everywhere."

"Well. Where do you like to be? What's your favorite place?"

He smiles and his body loses some of the tension. "I like walking my dog in the alley at sunset. We can see the whole city sprawled out. And Maurice likes to pee on all the trash cans."

"Your favorite place is a trash-filled alley full of dog pee?"

He turns to look at me, his gaze intense. "My favorite place is sitting with you, Eila Storm." He pauses. "But that's one of those things I say and then you'll feel uncomfortable, so I went with the alley."

My stomach tightens at the raw honesty of his words, at the way he just admits to his strong feelings for me. I decide to be honest right back. "I'm only uncomfortable because I'm not used to anyone being good to me."

We look at each other, neither of us saying anything more until a lightning bug lands on his leg and I hold out a finger. He watches as the bug crawls onto my hand and then flies away.

Ben sighs. "Can we talk about something else?"

I nod. "Sure. Whatever you want." I stare at the folder on the bench next to him. "Do we have enough light to finish those? You said you could get things moving with the lead test..."

"Oh. Sure. Yes." He grabs the folder and opens it. I lean in closer as we go through each of the questions, and the tops of our heads touch as we work on the forms together. I'm surprised to realize I don't hate the feeling, this closeness. Despite the heat, I'm comfortable here on this metal bench making progress toward my master plan.

We get to the end of the third page and Ben digs a pen from his pocket. "Black ink for the signature, Ms. Storm."

"Wouldn't want to break one of the rules about pen color." I nudge him with my shoulder and sign the paper quickly, staring down at it. "It's all happening now, huh?"

He grins. "It's all happening." I look into his eyes, glittering from the streetlamp overhead. I swallow, realizing that there's more happening here than just paperwork. I snap up to my feet, feeling vulnerable.

"Well, thanks for the assist. Can I text you if the lead stuff is confusing?"

"Please do. Call me when they drop off the kit, okay?"

I nod, backing down the street toward my house, wondering what I've gotten myself into.

13

BEN

THIS EVENING HAS ME UNSETTLED. It's not just the bowling alley incident. I'm used to freaking out in public. There's something extra happening where I'm freaking out in front of a woman I like, and she's totally fine with it. And I don't know what to make of any of it.

With only a few hours left before my alarm sounds for my workday, I lie back in my bed, listening to the air conditioner, petting my dog. I don't know if I fall asleep, but I enter this deeply relaxed state where I'm watching scenes from my life unfold. Every time I freaked out at the movies and shuffled out, sometimes leaving a date behind, ghosting her out of embarrassment.

Every time I couldn't handle the cafeteria in high school and ate my packed lunch in the loading dock, hoping I'd be able to sneak back through the custodians' door before the bell.

And tonight, when I was on the verge of sprinting from that bowling alley, but instead of rolling her eyes and calling me weird, Eila touched my arm with just the right amount of pressure and walked me outside.

My therapist is encouraging me to note these moments, these habits, these responses so we can start to work out a plan of interventions. It's so incredible to me that there might be a stable of tools and strategies to make these aspects of my life more manageable. What's even more incredible is the way that Eila Storm seems to know the secrets.

I POUR myself an extra mug of coffee in the morning and head downtown for a team meeting before I plan to drop Eila's paperwork directly into the hands of the director for the vacant lot program. Of course, when I reach that floor, I learn the director has taken another job in the private sector, and there are a bunch of frustrated city planning employees shuffling around that workload.

I frown. This isn't an unusual thing. But now it's impacting someone I care about, and I feel deeply conflicted knowing I could bend rules and make calls ... but once I cross that line I fear—no, I know I wouldn't be able to control myself. I'd spiral. Where does it end... if I break rules for Eila? No, better to hand her paperwork to one of the interns and watch it disappear into a stack, like all the other people applying for the same programs, with the same hopes and the same dreams as Eila Storm.

Except there is no one like Eila. There is no one who sees me uncomfortable and suggests alternatives. I stare at the overflowing inbox on the intern's desk until she looks up from her computer and lifts one ear of her headphones. "What's up?"

I cough and shift my weight. "I have an application for the lot program. But I guess Meryl left..."

The woman nods and rolls her eyes. "Yeah. Is it someone you know? I can process it after this press release." She looks at the papers. "Oh, this is a short one. Here." She pulls a stamp from her drawer and flips open a red ink pad. Before I can point out that she hasn't read the application, she inks a bright APPROVED on the top of the page. "Do me a favor and hand that to Naomi? She'll take it from there."

I back away from the desk with the paper, blinking and nodding, hoping Naomi is somehow related to lead testing.

There's no way it can be this easy for Eila to move ahead with her vision. I work for and in the system, and I know how long everything takes even with someone shepherding the paperwork along. But I realize, as I tuck the forms to the back of my clipboard, that I feel no anxiety about doing this favor for Eila. I consult the staff directory and make my way to Naomi's office, where I find a woman seated at an ancient desk, nearly hidden by a towering stack of boxes marked LEAD TEST: SOIL and LEAD TEST: WATER.

I clear my throat to announce my presence and hear the rattling voice of a seasoned smoker say, "Yeah? Who's there?"

"Yes. Hi. I'm Ben Barber from city inspections. I've got a lot adoption form approved to move to lead testing..."

"Soil or water? Actually, you know what? Take one of each. Instructions are inside."

A wrinkled hand nudges the top box from each tower, falling into my hands as Naomi spins around in her chair to answer the phone on her desk.

14

EILA

I'M HALFWAY through watering my fledgling hops when I hear shoes scuffing up the steps to my porch. I grin, knowing Ben has arrived with the lead testing kits. I know he hates that I'm already growing my hops without permission, but I can't just sit home all day watering my shower plants. Like I told Eden, the bines deter mites from her beehives. It's really a service that I'm doing this.

I set down my watering can just as a loud crash followed by shattering glass echoes from my front stoop. I whip around to find Ben sprawled awkwardly across the uneven porch steps, various boxes and papers scattered around him.

"Oh my god, are you okay?" I rush over, unable to contain my amusement at his flustered expression.

"Yeah, sorry, I just...there's no handrail and I

didn't realize..." Ben scrambles to collect the equipment, cheeks flaming.

A few empty pots shattered with his fall, and I gently extract a shard of ceramic from his palm. "Here, let me help."

He sucks in a breath when I touch him, and I apologize. "Sorry. I have this thing where I laugh when people fall down. I can't help it."

Ben shakes his head. "No, it's not that."

He stares as I rub the palm of his hand, looking for any additional shards. "Did I hurt you?"

"Not that either." My cheeks heat as I remember that Ben declared an intent to "woo" me, and now I'm squatting here on my porch with his hand pressed to my bare thigh.

I stand up and reach for the porch broom. He gathers the testing kits and I sweep up the debris. As I dump it into the trash bin off the side of the porch, an indignant squeak sounds from the porch rafters. Before I can react, the bat nesting under the eaves takes flight directly into Ben's startled face.

He cries out, swatting at the agitated creature. I shoo the bat away as Ben inspects his scalp.

"Um, I think you're bleeding a little there," I say, peering at the red scratch.

Ben pales. "Do you think it broke skin?" His voice pitches high with anxiety. "There's a not insignificant chance that bat had rabies."

I wince. "Oh, buddy. I definitely know you're supposed to call the CDC if a bat touches you. There was a whole thing last year with my sister Eliza and her goat barn."

Ben starts breathing rapidly. "How quickly do symptoms set in? Shit. Rabies is 100% fatal, Eila." He bends over, clutching his thighs, huffing and puffing.

I grab his uninjured hand, tugging him toward his car. "Let's not panic yet. You've got health insurance, right?"

Ben looks up, brow furrowed. "Of course I have health insurance."

I smirk at him. "Don't say it like everyone does. I don't. Anyway, Mr. Benefits, since you have the good coverage we can probably get you the shots pretty easily."

"Shots?" He pales and ducks his head back between his knees. "Ooooooh, god, no I hate shots."

I glance up at the eaves, where there is no further noise and no sign of the bat. "Well, we're not going to be able to catch the bat to test *it* for rabies, so I think you're going to have to suck it up, Ben. Come on, we'll go get you checked out."

We both decide it's better if I drive his car and Ben sits in the passenger seat with his forehead against the window as I blast the AC and distract him by listing all the amazing benefits of hops plants. "There's such a narrow harvest window, but the aroma when the flowers are ripe ... let me tell you, it's heavenly. Even if you don't drink beer."

He keeps his eyes closed and says, "You know I do enjoy beer."

"Well, then you're going to love how my yard smells in a few weeks."

"I will not be trespassing to sniff your illegal plants."

I snort out a laugh and merge onto Boulevard of the Allies toward Mercy Hospital.

At the emergency department, we check in and a bubbly blonde nurse named Stacia ushers Ben away toward the triage cubicle after a few flirtatious winks in his direction. He shoots me a helpless look over his shoulder that morphs into a frightened yelp when Stacia holds up a thermometer. He seems really overwhelmed by the emergency department. Or the threat of potential rabies. Or all of it. Wanting to comfort him, I walk toward him and hesitate, not sure if I'm allowed. "Can my friend come in here with me please?" Ben's words come out in a rush and the nurse nods. I hurry into the cubicle, squatting on the floor beside him.

"She's just checking your vitals, Ben." I try to communicate to Stacia with my eyes that Ben is pretty anxious about this entire situation. The man is high strung on a good day and now he's convinced he's going to die of rabies.

The trauma nurses here are used to gunshot victims and stab wounds, so Ben's run-in with the bat either doesn't ignite their sympathy or else they're super ready for a shift change. Stacia's eyes linger on Ben's forearms as he clutches the edge of his chair and I note that the man has some pretty nice veins and musculature happening there. But now isn't the time to be staring at them. Instead, I stroke his hand with my fingers, like I'm petting a feral cat.

"He's going to need the rabies vaccine series," I snap at the nurse. "And he wants to do the follow up shots at urgent care rather than keep coming back to the ED."

Ben turns to me. "Follow up shots?"

I pat his hand. "It's a whole thing, Ben. But you can do it. I know it."

By the time Stacia leaves to deal with vaccine paperwork, Ben is sweating. He's got the hospital gown folded on his lap and seems to be resisting putting it on as if that will prevent him from having to get shots up and down each thigh.

"You gonna put that on? Want me to step out?"

Ben flashes me a look of such anguish that I'm worried he has a physical injury he's not telling me about. "What's up, Ben? I promise I'll hold your hand during the shot. I don't need to look while you change..."

He closes his eyes and shakes his head. "It's not that. I mean, it is that. But...I really need to check on Maurice."

"Maurice?"

He swallows. "My dog? He's home alone, he could be out of water or needing to go out..." He rambles anxiously about his dog until I grasp his trembling hands.

"Hey, do you want me to go check on him?"

"Would you?" Ben's eyes water, like checking on a dog is some sort of heroic act.

"Sure. Give me back your keys and tell me what to do."

He hands me a tidy keyring and sinks back into the chair, visibly more relaxed.

"You sure you don't want me to stay while you get the shots?"

Ben presses his lips together and swallows. "I'd much rather you check on the dog and leave me to my suffering in private."

"Private? You mean with Nurse Stacia?"

Ben's jaw drops. "Are you implying that the staff will be inappropriate?"

I grin at him. "They better not be. Okay, I'm gonna go feed the dog and I'll swing right back for you, okay?"

Ben's shoulders slump in relief. "Thank you, Eila." He squeezes my fingers before pulling his polo shirt over his head. The last thing I see is his hairy, taut stomach, which is the moment I realize that I desperately want to run my fingers through that dark mess of fur.

I dart through the halls of the hospital with that image in my mind, cheeks flushed. Since when am I that attracted to Ben? I remind myself that we're friends now and I have to find his place and feed his dog.

I plug Ben's address into the maps app on my phone and enjoy the view as I make my way up the hill to his Greenfield townhouse. Of course, his grass is neatly trimmed but his yard is barren of all interesting plants. All that's on his front porch is a shoe brush, which I go ahead and use before I unlock his door.

I'm greeted by a mangy, weird-looking dog who does indeed have three legs. "Hey, you must be Maurice." I sink to my knees and offer my hand for him. "Obviously I'm not your dad. But he sent me."

The dog sniffs me and looks at me curiously. He's so old, I wonder if he can actually see my face. "So, I'm going to check on your water bowl and take you outside for a poo."

I walk through the living room, unsurprised by the lack of furniture but blown away by the presence of a piano along the far wall. I would never have expected Ben to be a musician, but I'm not sure why. Maybe because all the musicians I've dated have been pot-heads, and Ben is the furthest thing from that.

I spy Maurice's bowls in the kitchen and dump out the water in his dish, filling it from the filtered water in the fridge door. "This is high class, Maurice. Fridge water." When Esther installed a fridge with built-in water and ice, we all agreed that we had truly made it.

Maurice laps at the water and I look out Ben's windows. This neighborhood is peaceful during the day, the only sounds coming from a few far-off kids shrieking outside. It suits Ben, the stark contents of his home purely functional and clearly meant for just one person.

I dig the dog's leash and harness from the table inside the front door as instructed and turn to the dog, who must have heard the telltale sounds and tottered over to me. "You ready to go out?"

He yips. I grin and slip the contraption onto him, gingerly. "I think Ben is wrong," I tell him. "You'd look adorable in sporting wear." If I weren't unemployed, I might even go buy him a sweater set from Heather's shop. I'm certain he'd look dapper in it.

I open the front door and worry that Maurice

won't be able to hop down the steps, but that concern is quickly suppressed as he tugs me forward, ready to charge along what is clearly a well-known route. We head for the alley behind Ben's house, Maurice stopping to pee on a lot of different bushes and utility poles along the way.

He stops to do his business in the grass at the corner, and I bag it all up and urge him toward home. "I'm sure you usually do more stuff, but I have to go back and get your old man." Maurice yips, looking frustrated. I wish I could bring him with me to go back and fetch Ben, but I can't take him into the hospital and it's much too hot to leave him in the car while I wait for Ben to be discharged. "Sorry, dude. I'll have him back to you really soon, okay?"

I snap a picture of Maurice wagging his tail and send it to Ben, locking up the house and heading back toward Mercy hospital.

15

BEN

I STARE at the picture of my dog, my entire body clenched as I wait for the series of shots. The nurse said I'll need six pokes in each thigh for something that sounded like "immune goblins" and I can't get past the image of tiny monsters biting at my cells as the needles invade my body. Should I have told the nurse I'm autistic? Would that have changed my care in a positive way?

I take a deep breath and I hear her approach, wheeling a metal cart. "All right, Mr. Barber." She winks. Is Eila right that the nurse is flirting with me? That seems inappropriate, but maybe she has a thing for men who can't handle shots. I grit my teeth and bear it when I'm due for a tetanus booster, but most years I don't even get the flu shot. I just really cannot stand the thought of being ... pierced.

I should have studied biomedical engineering and developed some new method to deliver these kinds of medications.

Nurse Stacia has a tray with a baker's dozen needles lined up and a stack of alcohol wipes. "First I'll clean the area," she says as she wipes the wet pad along my leg. The disinfectant evaporates quickly, making me shiver. I am deeply uncomfortable, but I know I have to do this. Or do I? I begin to calculate the probability that the bat was rabid ... but then I remember that rabies is 100% fatal. Yes, I need to go through with this. I'm still doing math with my eyes squeezed shut when I feel the pinch of the first shot. I shriek.

"Sorry," Stacia says without looking. She jabs the second shot into my leg a few inches from the first injection site.

I grip the edge of the gurney and stare at the ceiling. I know I'm groaning and I'm actively forcing myself not to rock back and forth as the jabs keep on coming. "Can you relax your legs at all, Ben? This will hurt less if you can ease up the tension..."

I shake my head, unable to contemplate adjusting anything at all about my posture. Then I hear a welcome sound. Eila is back. I turn to the hall and see her dark head as she hurries toward me. "I'm here! Did you see the picture I sent? Oh, poor Ben."

Eila crosses the threshold and sees Stacia get started on my second leg. I keep my eyes glued to Eila as she crosses the room and stands by my side. I smell her, sunshine and green things, and begin to relax ever so slightly. She squeezes my hand, face awash with sympathy. I think that's what it is. Eila doesn't seem like the sort of person to pity people.

I let my head sink to her shoulder, she wraps an arm around my face, shielding my eyes. The shots hurt less. Or the shock of them bothers me less, at any rate.

"Just the arm left," comes Stacia's voice and I feel the cold of the alcohol wipe on my left deltoid. I know I'm moaning into Eila's shoulder, but she doesn't seem to mind. She starts stroking my hair and I want to sink into that sensation, revel in the scent and warmth of her.

A few moments pass and I peel myself away to see Stacia has left the room. Confused, I furrow my brow and look around. Eila tosses me my jeans. "She went for your paperwork. You want me to turn around while you get dressed?"

I shake my head and tug on my pants, shedding the gown to put my polo back on and then running my fingers through my hair to try and settle it down from whatever mess it's become.

"You feeling, okay?" Eila looks at the floor and I see her cheeks are pink. I wonder if she likes anything about the sight of me half naked. Do I detect any sort of interest from her? Would I know how to proceed if she is interested?

"My legs hurt," I admit, and she looks up as I wince. "I hate this."

She reaches for my hand and squeezes. "Well, the good news is you won't die of rabies." I glance at our joined hands and can't help the smile breaking across my face. Tentatively, I interlace our fingers and my heart stumbles. Eila squeezes and smiles back at me.

We sit in tired silence until someone else comes into the room with a pile of paperwork. "You're all set, Mr. Barber." The tech, whose name tag reads Anton, hands me my insurance card and a small card. "You can pop into the urgent care on Centre Ave in four days for the next shot."

I thank him and slide from the gurney, walking gingerly toward the exit, my hand still held tight in Eila's.

16

EILA

BEN DRIVES his own car away from the hospital and it doesn't occur to me to ask him to take me home. Which is how I wind up at his townhouse, following him up his porch steps and listening for the clickity-clack of Maurice's paws approaching the door.

"Hey, buddy." Ben's voice is very different when he's talking to his dog. "I'm here. Yes, I know I'm late." Ben gets the door open and immediately squats down to receive affection from his dog. I watch this uptight man who was afraid of needles revel in having his entire face licked by a mangy old dog and ... it does things to my pants.

Ben reaches past Maurice for the harness I left sitting out on the table, and I wait for Ben to comment on my sloppiness, but he just seems excited to be reunited with his hound. He grins up at me as he fastens the leash. "Want to come walk with us?"

I nod, not quite able to articulate why I feel overwhelmed by the sight of all this. It's not like I've never seen people with pets. Eliza has an entire herd of goats and a babysitter-donkey for them. But it's different with Ben. He's welcoming me into a very special partnership and it's intimate. Responsible. Ben Barber is a real adult, and I like that about him. Very much. Even as I realize I am inadequately un-adult by comparison. This man has his entire life together and I don't get why he seems so committed to helping me reroute mine.

He and Maurice amble slowly down the sidewalk toward the alley. It occurs to me that walking a three-legged dog at a snail's pace is the perfect antidote for Ben's sore legs from all the shots. I stuff my hands in my pockets and walk beside them, kicking gravel. I usually feel uncomfortable in silence like this, and I notice the absence of that discomfort right now. With Ben and Maurice, I feel ... still. It's nice.

Maurice raises a leg to pee on a trash can and we pause while he gets himself situated. Ben's eyebrows lift up and he turns to me. "Oh. We didn't do your lead collection."

I wave a hand. "That's okay. I'll do it tomorrow."

Ben presses his lips together, considering. "I

should have taken you home." He runs a hand through his hair. "I'm all out of sorts."

I punch him softly in the shoulder and then freeze when he winces. "Shit. Your shot. Anyway, I was going to say it's okay because, you know, I gave you rabies or whatever."

"Hm." Ben stoops to gather up Maurice, who started to dig in some garbage. We walk a bit and Ben sets the dog down near some grass at the corner. My breath catches when I look up and see the entire city sprawled below us, sparkling in the dark. All the lights of downtown shine against a clear sky with a bright, white moon.

"Wow."

Ben makes a pleased sound. When I look over at him, he's smiling, his face transformed with happiness. But he's not looking at our beautiful city. He's smiling at me.

I tuck my hair behind my ears and lick my lips. "I see why you like living up here."

"Best view of the city. But you being here definitely makes it prettier."

Both of us blush at his blatantly honest words of praise. "You can't just say things like that," I whisper.

"Why not? It's true. You're gorgeous, Eila Storm."

I breathe through my nose, trying to make sense of the hurricane inside my stomach. "I forgot you're planning to woo me."

He chuckles at my use of his weird word. "How am I doing?"

"Come on, Ben. I can't be wooed. You can't woo me. My life is a mess."

Maurice yaps at a firefly and lunges forward. We follow him into the park, letting him totter around nipping at bugs. Ben runs a hand along his cheek, like he's unhappy with how his skin feels. "I thought I was helping you iron things out with your side hustle."

"Side hustle? You mean the hops?" He nods. I snort. "I don't have a main hustle, Barber. This is it for me. All I've got going on."

"That's not true. You've got great sisters. You're calm in a crisis." He gestures to his legs.

"The bat incident hardly counts as a crisis."

"Well, it felt like it to me. And I benefited from your help with all that. I would have just laid on your porch freaking out if you hadn't been there."

I decide to stop arguing with him about it and glance up at the moon again. It really is a beautiful night. If Ben were a different person, I'd grab him by the shirt collar and kiss the hell out of him. I would drag him home and do all sorts of things with him, none involving soil collection. But Ben Barber isn't some guy I grab at a party to have my way with quickly and never talk to again.

He's proper and respectable and loves the shit

out of his dog and suddenly I want very much to be home in my chaotic plant-filled shower. "I'm going to check the bus schedule."

I pull out my phone and gasp when Ben rests a hand on mine, covering the screen. "Eila. I'm driving you home." His tone doesn't leave room for argument, so I nod. He whistles quietly for Maurice and spins back toward the house. Ben fishes his keys from his pocket and lifts the dog into the back seat of his car where, of course, he has some sort of dog car seat harness set up.

We drive in relative quiet, each of us only talking to Maurice, until Ben pulls up along the missing curb by my house. He glances up at the porch, where my sister has the light on for once. "Let's just grab the soil samples and I'll drop them off when I go to work tomorrow."

I turn to face him. "You're not afraid we'll step on a poisonous snake in the dark?"

He frowns at me. "Eila. First of all, snakes are *venomous*. And second, we have Maurice. He'd scare them all off."

I can't think of an argument for that, and I hurry up the steps to find the detritus of the lead kit from Ben's giant wipeout earlier. He pulls a small-but-powerful flashlight from his pocket to light our way and I quickly fill the sample container while Maurice supervises. I screw the lid on tightly and bite my lip, realizing as I hand the jar to Ben that I've become very invested in the results. Every instinct I have pushes me to run away from the possibility of getting shut down, to kick Ben out of the yard and try again off-grid with the lot across the street, paperwork be damned.

But then Maurice licks my ankle and Ben smiles at the sample, holding it up in the moonlight. And I worry a tiny bit less about the outcome.

17

BEN

I WINCE as the needle pierces my arm, hoping I don't audibly groan. I stare at the seaside poster on the wall, wondering if it actually helps calm other patients. I wish I had someone here with me for emotional support, and then grit my teeth at the idea of needing emotional support for a shot. The urgent care nurse, Kai, doesn't seem to notice my embarrassment as he sticks a bandage over the injection site. "All done, Mr. Barber." Kai drops the syringe in the sharps container and tosses his gloves in the trash.

I make a mental note to bring this all up with Dr. Morgan at our next session. I feel like my entire life has changed since I saw her last. I know she'd want me to think about what specifically is so upsetting right now—the smell of the alcohol wipe, sharp in the dry air of the clinic? The bright lights? The unknown person gripping my arm with unpredictable amounts of pressure? All of the above? Fuck it. I can't work through all this right now.

I realize Kai is waiting for me to say or do something. "Sorry," I mutter. "Can you repeat that?"

Kai smiles. "I was just saying take your time and you can schedule the next shot with the desk on your way out."

"Oh. Thank you." I move to rise from the chair and follow him, but my phone chimes in my pocket.

CASH

Haven't heard from you. How are
things with The One?

ME

Too much going on for a text.

CASH

Want to meet me at East End after
work? I'll have Ruby…

I like the brewery near Cash's house, not just because they serve really good beer but also because they allow dogs.

ME

Maurice and I will see you soon.

I hurry out of the urgent care clinic, looking forward to the icy IPA I'll reward myself with for enduring all this medical stuff.

I check my mailbox at work to see if anyone has returned the results from Eila's lead test and, seeing nothing but an empty cubby, hurry through the rest of my paperwork, eager to go and meet Cash.

Maurice and I arrive first, and I grab a picnic table and a few beers while Maurice settles in for a snooze under the table. I hear Ruby before I see her and Cash as the little girl squeals in delight at my tri-pawed pet. "Can I hug him?"

I nod and she darts under the table. Cash grins and sits across from me on the bench, gladly taking the glass I slide his way. He takes a few swigs and sighs. "That's good stuff. Hey, I was in the old neighborhood today installing solar panels."

I frown. "Someone must have moved or died. Nobody on our old block would invest in renewable energy."

Cash chuckles. "You said it, not me." He glances under the table to check on his daughter and hands her some money to go buy a soda from the bar. "So." Cash folds his arms on the table and looks me in the eye, not letting me ignore him. "You've been a-wooin'?"

"Knock it off. I regret using that word."

"I've been wondering if you were secretly

Amish." I frown and Cash laughs. "Go on. Tell me about the plant girl." I scowl more intensely, and he holds up his hands. "Woman. Plant woman."

I briefly explain that I tripped on her not-up-to-code porch and disturbed a bat while delivering the lead test kit and Cash laughs so hard he has to stand up and squeeze his legs to calm down.

"It's not funny. My legs are black and blue from the injections."

Ruby, hearing the commotion, returns from the bar with a soda and looks at her father. "What's funny?"

I point at her. "There's nothing funny about rabies. If you touch a bat, you'll need over 16 shots."

Ruby's eyes fly wide. "Sixteen?"

I nod. "I still have two to go."

Cash drops an arm around her shoulders and kisses the top of her head. "And that's why we don't touch wild animals and always ask an adult before we pet a dog."

We all sip our drinks in silence for a bit, letting this advice settle in, until Cash asks, "But she walked your dog while you were getting stuck up like a pin cushion?" I nod. Cash beams. "That's great news, man. You need to make your move now, while she's feeling a little bad about the bat."

I furrow my brow and sip my drink. "That feels manipulative."

He leans forward. "You had her under the moonlight in close proximity, after she drove you to the hospital and walked your dog, and you didn't even go for a peck on the cheek?"

When he puts it that way, I feel foolish for not trying to kiss Eila. Was she expecting me to? Does she feel rejected? "I'm terrible at this. I'm always terrible with people."

Cash's girlfriend appears, smiling, kissing Cash and Ruby on the cheek before turning to me. "You are a little gruff, it's true. Did Cash just say you had a moonlight adventure?"

She sinks onto the bench next to my friend and they link hands. I stare at their entwined fingers, wondering if I'd ever feel comfortable just reaching for Eila, touching her that way. Cash's face shifts into such adoration, especially when Piper leans her head on his shoulder.

He presses a kiss to Piper's hair and tells her, "I was just telling Ben he needs to capitalize on the moment. Just go for it and kiss her already."

Piper smiles. "She already knows you're interested. That's the scariest part, I think. Admitting that."

I frown and notice my glass is empty. "She told me she doesn't want to be wooed."

Piper pats my hand. "Ben, nobody wants to be *wooed.*" She reaches for Cash's glass and finishes his beer in one swig. "You've got to knock her socks off so she can't resist you."

I groan. "Piper, I understand that *knock her socks off* is a thing people say." I don't want to use the word idiom here and sound weird. "Can you be more specific? I really appreciate the advice."

Piper smiles. "Have you heard the phrase love language?" I shake my head. I have, of course, *heard* this phrase, but I know she's asking if I know what it means. Which I don't. She adds, "People tend to respond to certain types of...wooing. Some people really like gifts. Some people really like to hear beautiful words of praise."

"I don't think I can offer that to anyone."

Piper taps the edge of the table, her face tight with concentration. "My guess is Eila's love language is acts of service." I blink, waiting for further explanation. "She will really like it if you do nice things for her."

I relax a bit. "I can do that."

Cash nods. Piper points finger guns at me. "Yeah, you can."

Cash gathers his little family and heads for home, gesturing for me to call him, presumably once I've made progress with Eila. I watch them walk away hand in hand, wondering how on earth a surly weirdo like me could ever seem irresistible to a woman like Eila Storm.

But if Piper is to be trusted, I don't need to worry about being attractive so much as I just need to keep doing nice things for her. And that seems almost too easy. Eila wants approval to grow hops on that vacant lot. I'm more determine than ever to make that happen for her.

18

EILA

I forgot today is Monday. All the days blend together now that I'm not working. I wake up to a dozen missed texts from my sisters and brother-in-law about family dinner and haul myself out of bed. I guess I'm cooking. Which is fair since what the hell else do I have to do while my hops project is in limbo and I'm unemployed.

Speaking of ... I peck around on Eden's laptop and rush through the application for unemployment. The last thing I need is to give my sisters more evidence that I'm a failure. Part of me knows that hops farmer isn't anyone's ticket to the upper class. But I'm used to living lean. I've stretched money before, and I can do it again.

Inspired, I vow to prepare family dinner on a shoestring budget. I take the bus down to the produce terminal building and buy a bunch of random things from the discount market. Warty carrots and misshapen peppers are way cheaper, and they all taste the same sliced and sauteed.

After my successful shopping trip, my bag is full and it's not sweltering, so I decide to walk over the Allegheny River to Esther's house on the north side of the city.

I let myself into my sister's house, wondering where they all are, and make myself busy watering her plants. How can she just let them all wilt like this? I know she's busy, but surely between her and Koa, one of them can dump a water glass into the spider plant now and then, right? And Eva is still living here, too, as far as I can tell.

I'm grouchy as I prune the crispy bits from the aloe and philodendron and I snap when I hear the door open, signaling the arrival of the entire Storm flock. "How can you just let these guys go like this? I gave you plants that require the bare minimum of care ..."

Esther arches a brow at me and shoves a bottle of wine into her husband's chest. He silently slinks into the kitchen, presumably to put it in the fridge and let Esther rip me a new one.

She points to the couch, and I roll my eyes as I sink into the cushions. "Eila." She pats my leg. Eva, Eden, and Eliza all sit beside her. They're like a row of nesting dolls, staring at me behind curtains of dark hair and darker eyes. "You are not okay, love."

I throw my hands in the air. "No shit I'm not okay." Esther's face pinches and I wince. "Sorry. But ... yeah. I'm not okay. And neither are your plants."

Esther inhales through her nose. "Plants aside, tell us what's going on with you. I thought you'd have a new job by now ... it never takes you this long in between gigs."

And that's the entire problem. My entire resume is just one dead-end job after another. They're all gigs. There's nothing I'm proud of, nothing that revs my engine like Bridges and Bitters does for Esther or the damn goats do for Eliza. Until this project I've got going.

"I'm doing the hops thing," I whine. "It's just taking a while."

Eden frowns. "Didn't you say it would be three years minimum for that to earn a profit?"

Confused, Esther leans back. Her posture is more relaxed now and I feel my own shoulders sink a tiny bit. Esther licks her teeth. "I don't think I fully understand the *hops thing*. Can you tell me exactly what you've got cooking?"

I wave a hand. "I'm taking over the vacant lot by our house and planting hops. It's a win-win for everyone since they help prevent erosion, the bines deter mites for Eden's bees, and a lot of the breweries nearby are into sourcing things local."

Esther's clock ticks loudly in the silence while she gathers her thoughts. "What sort of yield can you get from one lot?"

I stare at my knees. "It's an extremely valuable crop."

Esther reaches for my chin and tips it up, so I meet her gaze. "How many lots would you need to grow enough and sell enough for this to be your only source of income?"

I swat her hand away. "None of you ever believe me that I've done my research on this. It's a viable project, okay?"

Esther closes her eyes and rubs at her temples. "I do believe you, honey. I am trying to talk through the logistics, listen to your business plan."

My stomach clenches. "I don't need to provide you with a business plan, Esther. I spent enough time figuring all that shit out for the stupid permit process."

There's a long silence and the five of us just sort of breathe angrily. I can feel the moment Esther decides to let it go—for now at least—and she stands up. "What are we making for dinner? I'm starving."

We cook together, me brooding and them gabbing about work and potholes and Koa's haircut. Usually all the nonsense feels cozy but today it feels pointed and directed at me. All of them are gainfully employed. None of them are fuckups who get fired and concoct questionably-legal schemes to earn a living outside the norm.

I'm silent all through dinner and during the ride home in Eden's van. Eventually, Eden clicks her tongue and asks, "Do I need to worry about your share of the rent? Did you get the unemployment set up at least?"

I don't look at her when I say, "You'll get the rent money."

I know I have to do something to keep myself alive while I sort all this out. I can't explain my urge to wallow in this project any more than I can explain why I mouthed off to one customer too many and got fired in the first place. But I also know I'm not going to abandon this plan just because it seems doomed. All I've ever known is people leaving me and my sisters behind when the going got tough. I'll figure something out.

Eden doesn't look like she believes me, though.

I'm relieved when I hear my phone chime with an incoming text, because I have an excuse to turn my attention away from my sister.

STRANGER BEN

Hey, it's Ben.

ME

I have you in my phone. You don't
have to introduce yourself each
time you text me.

STRANGER BEN

Right. Sorry.

Can you give me a call?

I frown at my sister as she parks in front of our house. "Hey," I ask her. "Can I borrow your car?" She shrugs and hands me the keys. I pull out my phone and respond to Ben.

ME

I'll just come over. See you in ten.

19

BEN

She's coming over. To my house. I look at Maurice. "She's coming over."

He licks my leg. What does he know about it?

I showed up at work today and saw the lead kit results on my desk. I should have called Eila immediately, shared the good news with her about the soil beside her house.

I don't know why I sat on the news, waffled all day about the perfect way to convey the information. And now she's coming over to hear it from me in person.

Should I clean? I glance around my house. Everything is already pretty tidy. My mom would probably light one of those scented candles, but those give me a headache. I don't really think Eila's into that sort of thing anyway.

I grab the broom and furiously sweep the floor, and then I notice some swirls of dog hair blowing around so I grab the handheld vacuum instead, along with my noise canceling headphones that hang on a hook beside the vacuum. I frantically suck up every speck of fur floating in my living room and tell myself that will have to do when it comes to prepping for my visit from Eila.

I sit on the floor and scratch Maurice's belly while I wait for her to arrive and, an eternity later, I hear a soft tap on the door. I must fly over to open it too quickly because she rears her head back when I pull the door in with a rush.

"Sorry." I'm always apologizing. I need to work on that. I'm allowed to be here and I'm allowed to be who I am. It's okay to be different from other people. If I repeat these mantras enough, my therapist assures me I will begin to believe them.

Eila shrugs and steps inside, stooping to greet Maurice, which sets me more at ease. "What's up?" She lifts her brows.

Since she's already down low with the dog, I sit on the floor with both of them, smiling. "You do not have excessive levels of lead in your soil. Well. The city's soil. Your lot is okay."

Her face brightens and she brings her hands up to her mouth. "Are you serious?"

"I'm always serious," I tease, and she pushes my shoulder, laughing.

"That's incredible, Ben. Thank you." She stands up and jumps up and down a few times, chanting *yes, yes, yes*. "I really needed that news today."

She looks around the room, looking for somewhere to sit. But I've only got the one chair and the piano bench, so she just sits back down with me and Maurice on the floor.

"You had a bad day?"

She nods. "More like a bad … life? Bad couple of years? Anyway, I needed a win."

"Hm." I don't like hearing her talk this way about her challenges. It worries me. One thing I do know about myself is that I get very fixated on my worries when they involve people I care about. And I care about Eila Storm. "Want to talk about it?"

Eila seems to consider this. Eventually, she says, "I really don't. Thank you, though. You know my whole..." She waves a hand around. "You know my situation. And for some reason you're on board to help me with this hare-brained scheme, so that tells me it can't be too awful of an idea."

"What makes you say that?"

She smiles. "You aren't the kind of guy who pursues anything hare-brained."

"I guess that's fair. And accurate. And you don't mind that? Me being serious all the time?"

Her smile widens and my stomach flips at the sight. "I mind enough to tease you about it. But no, Ben. Of course I don't mind. You're just being you."

How long have I waited to find someone who sees me just being myself and ... appreciates that rather than finds it weird or off-putting? My own mother has worked herself into fits trying to change the parts of me that Eila seems to accept without question. I think back to my conversation with Cash, how he encouraged me to go big and be bold with this woman. I blow out a breath, steeling myself.

"Eila." I touch her hand. It's warm and firm and sturdy. "You know I'm wild about you, right?"

She nods her head. "Yes. The wooing. You've mentioned it." She turns her hand over in mine and squeezes.

I have no idea how to read this signal from her and I want to growl and scream and lunge at her... I close my eyes and ask, "Can I kiss you?"

20

EILA

My heart beats so fast and so hard, I swear I can hear it. Ben looks at me intently, waiting for an answer, and his lip trembles a bit, like whatever I say might either save him or destroy him. I swallow a thick knot in my suddenly-dry throat.

"It's not that I don't want to kiss you, Ben. If you were anyone else, I'd fuck you senseless."

His eyes widen and I hear him suck in a breath. "Anyone else? But not me?"

I close my eyes and press a palm to my chest as if I could somehow slow the racing drumbeat inside. "Anyone else, because once I sleep with someone, I don't stick around. Maybe I'll try it once or twice more, but I can't afford to be getting emotionally attached to someone and, frankly, the sex really isn't terrific with random guys. I always think, each time, that it'll be somehow satisfying or fill some sort of emptiness."

I watch Ben's throat move as he swallows. His leg starts to shake as he listens to me talk. I can feel him resisting the urge to touch me.

"Do you get what I'm saying at all?"

He shakes his head. "I have no idea what you're getting at. I hear you saying you've been having bad sex."

I spit out a burst of uncomfortable laughter. "It's not *bad.* It's just not awesome like romance novel sex, or something."

Ben clasps his thighs so tightly I can see the veins rise in his hands. "Eila, you should be having mind-blowing sex. You deserve to be worshiped."

I inch a bit away from him, shaking my head. "You can't say things like that, Ben. This is what I'm talking about. I care about you. We're friends. And I'm dark and broken inside and I can't do more than that. Which also means I'm not going to fuck you, because that wouldn't be right."

"Eila. I didn't ask you to fuck me. I just asked if I could kiss you." He lifts a hand slightly, like he wants to reach for me, but decides against it.

I shake my head again, harder this time. "It's too much, kissing. Too serious."

"I'm seriously infatuated with you, Eila. I'm very serious about it."

"Yeah, Ben, but I can't do that. I can't be serious about someone. I can't let myself trust you, or fucking *need* you. Because any time I need someone, they crush me. Do you know what that's like? To let yourself need your mom, to hope she might turn up for the science fair like she said she would and then you're just standing there like an asshole with your shitty cardboard project as everyone else's mom smiles and pats your arm?"

"Eila, I'm not—"

"No. I'm just not strong enough to go through something like that, to crave you and your dumb ugly dog and have you fuck up and ruin me. Because you will, Ben. Everyone does."

He closes his eyes. "There's no reason to bring Maurice into this."

"Ha." This time my laughter is a little more genuine. "Okay. I'm sorry I insulted Maurice."

"He'd never let you down, you know. He never would do that." On cue, the dog pops his head up from his tuffet and begins licking my ankle.

"Well," I look down at him. "I guess Maurice can kiss me, then."

"I'm so sorry you've been through all that, Eila. I don't know what to say except...I've been let down before, too. And I've felt alone, too. And when I'm with you, I don't know. I just feel seen in a way I can't really describe. And I don't want to pressure you to do anything you don't want to do, but it also feels important to tell you how much I admire you and—"

He stops talking and his eyes flash with something I can't identify. Possession? Ferocity? He takes a deep breath that shudders on his exhale. "We don't have to kiss. I'm sorry I pressured you. But if you wanted to do something less intimate, I'm happy to celebrate with you however you feel comfortable."

I furrow my brow and cross my arms. "Less intimate than making out? What do you even mean?"

He shrugs. "We could get a beer. Or I could give you a hug."

"I thought you don't like people touching you."

Ben shakes his head almost violently. "I don't like how other people touch me. I very much like to touch you."

"Well how's that work?" He shrugs and I roll my eyes. "Fine."

"Fine what?"

I hold my hands palm up in surrender. "Fine, you can hug me. Let's try it. I'm in."

I try not to focus on the wave of embarrassment

rushing through me that I don't really know how to hug someone. Who has ever hugged me? Esther for sure when she's had time. My other sisters, I guess. But other people? Physical contact has always come with expectations. But when Ben Barber leans forward and wraps his arms around me, it's another thing entirely. He rests his chin on my shoulder, feeling his breath against my ear. I can feel his heart pounding in his chest, too. He trembles slightly and then squeezes me a bit tighter. His arms are strong and powerful, gentle and liquid yet also the most solid thing I've ever felt.

And despite always feeling uncomfortably sweaty and hot, I don't mind the heat of this embrace he's giving me. Soon, I begin to sink into him, resting my cheek against his shoulder. "Wow," I whisper, not deliberately. I should be embarrassed, but I shudder and settle in, just enjoying this moment.

"Umm." I feel his chest vibrate as he emits a satisfied humming sort of sound, pulling his arms a bit tighter around me. So, this is a hug. A real, affectionate embrace.

I don't know how long he hugs me before I brave movement. I inch my arms from my sides to his, snaking my hands slowly around his back and feeling him beneath my palms. But I don't slide my hands into his pants or reach for his ass. I just...hold him as he holds me.

We breathe in unison until I realize this is even more dangerous than fucking. Even more intimate than kissing. This is me literally leaning on Ben Barber, and as quickly as I sank into the hug, I draw back. *Not safe*, my heart seems to chant. *Too much.*

21

BEN

When Eila pulls out of my arms, I can feel all my nerve endings yearning for her. I realize fully that she has become what my therapist refers to as my special interest.

Eila sets my body at ease as much as she lights my skin on fire. But I can tell that what we've done just now—gentle hugging for crying out loud—has upset her.

She scoots back to the edge of the bench, and I wait for her to talk. When she doesn't, I blurt out all the words pressing against my frontal lobe. "You calm me down where the rest of the humans on this planet confuse me, Eila. You just seem to instinctively know how to touch me and ... set me at ease. Do you understand how rare that is? How special?"

I see tears well up in her eyes and she shakes her head. "Don't say those things, Ben."

I throw my hands in the air. "Why? What's so awful about someone appreciating your goodness, Eila? I'm not saying I think you're perfect. Recall that you're a serial trespasser and you live in a house that does not in any way meet city building code specifications."

That gets a smile from her and the victory of making her feel better feels like a shining light I wish I could squeeze. Rhythmically, until my heart rate settles.

She licks those incredible lips and presses her hands into her thighs. "I need to go home. This has all been a lot and I'm probably going to take illegal drugs and go to sleep."

I arch a brow. "Should I be worried?"

She laughs and lightly punches my shoulder. "I'm talking about funny honey, not propofol, goof." She must sense my confusion because she explains, "Eden's beekeeping mentor steeps backyard marijuana in honey. A few drops on the tongue and all your racing worries drift away...and you can sleep."

I consider this. "I didn't know you had racing worries or trouble sleeping."

She shrugs. "Unemployment doesn't typically lead to restful slumber. Does it? Anyway, not for me."

I know Eila grew up without much security. I'm not surprised to learn it impacts her like this. I also know she'd probably benefit from the kind of mental health support I'm getting … but Eila has been pretty clear that she doesn't have health insurance. I swallow. "Well, sweet dreams, I guess."

She grins. "Was that a joke about the honey?"

I laugh. "I hadn't thought of that."

"Most guys would take the credit for being clever."

"I told you, Eila Storm, there's nothing regular about me."

I ACTUALLY DO STRUGGLE to fall asleep after I walk her to her car and watch her drive off in her sister's van. If I close my eyes, I can still feel the heat of her body in my arms. The weight of her head pressed against my shoulder. The slight tickle of her hair against my chin.

I text Cash an update:

> Reminded Eila I'm all-in for her.
> We hugged.

I wake up to his reply:

Is a hug a good thing? Man, I was
rooting for you to get a kiss at
least.

ME:

I'm okay with the hug.

CASH:

For now, right?

ME:

For now.

22

EILA

I'm surprised to find Eden awake when I get home from Ben's, shaken up by emotion and over-whelmed by the intensity of the stupid (okay, incredible) hug. "What's up?" I hang her van keys on the hook, and she sighs.

"The rent is due, sis."

My cheeks heat. "Shit." I sink onto the couch and drag my fingers through my hair. "I didn't get my unemployment figured out yet."

Eden taps her toe. "It's been a few weeks, though...what about your last check from the nursery?"

I shrug. "What do you want me to say? It wasn't much and I spent it on groceries." I feel myself getting defensive and I know that's not fair. My sister didn't ask for this burden. It's not like either of us has some designer cushion for times like these. "I'll go to the office in East Liberty tomorrow. See if I can get it sorted."

Eden nods. She doesn't remind me that our landlord tends to cash checks immediately, that we can't just write one for the full amount and hope we have a few days to actually put the money in our shared account. If it were up to me, I probably wouldn't have a bank account at all.

Esther says that's my poverty talking. The whole thing baffles me, so Esther's probably right about that. Eden and I learned the hard way that having a bank account and giving people access to withdraw from it just leads to fees upon fees.

I glance up at my sister, feeling contrite. "Maybe you'll get a call for a big swarm removal or something…"

She smiles and sniffs out a laugh through her nose. "The second I do, I'm spending the excess on a massage. I hauled a few tons of honey around today."

"Sounds lucrative."

Eden slaps the Newell post and heads up the stairs. She says over her shoulder, "It'd better be."

I set my alarm extra early and catch the first bus toward the unemployment office near the Home Depot. There's always a line before it opens, a sea of people who can't get their health insurance benefits sorted or figure out the proper paperwork for their unemployment. Like me. I am the huddled masses or however the saying goes on the Statue of Liberty. Not that I've ever seen it.

I tug a hat on to fight the sun and allow myself to wallow a bit. I've never left Pittsburgh apart from a trek up Route 79 to the hops farm in nearby Slippery Rock. I'm unemployed. I'm a burden on all my sisters.

The line moves quickly, and I grit my teeth. I can figure this out. I've done it before. I'm actually not sure why there's a holdup. I can get this sorted out, pay the rent and then some. I can live lean until my hops harvest in a few months. If I hadn't gotten the plants started illegally, I'd have to wait an entire year. But I was just squirrely enough to eke through this mess.

"Next."

A woman named Devorah frowns at me beneath bushy gray eyebrows, her dark skin looking dreary in the flickering lights of this office. "Hi. I'm Eila Storm. I'm having trouble accessing my unemployment compensation."

I slide my driver's license toward her with a

smile. She glances at it and looks back at me, expression unchanged. "Social security number?"

I recite the number to her, and she clacks around on her computer for probably seventeen minutes before she sighs and says, "There's no active case for you. Try filing again and make sure you have all the correct details from your former employer."

"No active case? I applied over a week ago and--"

Devorah seems not to hear me. She's already looking behind me, to the huge line of people with crying babies. "Next."

A woman with a baby lashed to her chest and another clinging to her leg approaches the folding chair and I stand, reaching for my license. I will not cry. This is a solvable problem.

It's faster to walk to the nursery than wait for a bus, so I stomp down Penn Avenue toward Shady, fully intending to scream at my boss. He must be declining my request, I decide. It's the only logical explanation for this. And that pisses me off, because it's one thing to fire me and another thing entirely to essentially rob me of any ability to pay rent and keep a roof over my head while I get back on my feet.

I'm in a proper lather when I pass the pet store, but I halt on the sidewalk because I see Ben, smiling ridiculously broadly in a way that seems foreign on his usually stern face. He must sense my mood, which means I'm upset enough that even this guy who has trouble knowing what people are feeling can read my nonverbal cues. "Eila." He sets a sack of pet food on the sidewalk and approaches me. "What's wrong?"

I close my eyes. I should be able to just calmly tell him that the rent is due, and I can't seem to figure out how to pay it. But I'm worried he'd offer to front me the money and then I'd feel beholden to him and sleep with him and it would be terrible and then I wouldn't have him helping me anymore. And then, I remember how I felt in his arms and for some reason that embarrasses me more than my failure to obtain unemployment compensation and I'm just overcome by all of it, plus now I can smell Ben's laundry detergent and feel the warmth seeping from him as he reaches for me.

"Hey." He runs a palm down my arm. It feels nice. "You're shaking."

I glance down at my body and realize he's right. He tips his head toward his car. "Come sit. I'll blast the AC."

I shake my head. "You can't idle here. It's a no idle zone. The plants are breathing."

Ben laughs. "Okay then." He glances up and down the street. "Come sit on the curb with me? Over there in the shade?" He pops open the hatch on his car and tosses the dog food inside, then walks across the street.

I nod and follow him, sinking onto the sidewalk and barely caring that we look like vagrants. He angles his body so he's facing me. "What happened?"

It's easier than I expected to just tell him I can't figure out my unemployment paperwork. The next thing I know, I'm sitting at the counter in a coffee shop leaning against Ben's firm body as he clacks around on his laptop. "Here, I'll close my eyes while you type your information." He squeezes his eyes shut and I bite back a laugh at how serious he is, even when he's doing something super nice for me. "Don't worry about the public Wi-Fi, either. We're using a hotspot from my phone. It's very secure."

I chuckle as I type in the numbers. "It would never have occurred to me to worry about that. Thank you, though. Here."

Ben nods and pokes around the form a few times, refreshing the browser a lot and grunting. "That's how I feel every time I access that state portal."

He growls at the screen. "This is worse than the city website. And that's saying something." I smile, feeling a little better that someone as capable as Ben is also struggling with the website. "You'd think I'd be better at this after helping my mom. But I think they changed everything."

I slurp my drink. "You helped your mom with this stuff?"

He nods but doesn't look away from the screen. "Not since I turned 18. But yeah." He clacks the keys triumphantly and points at the screen. "Aha. You have a different address." I rest my chin on his shoulder. I don't know why, but I like it. I can smell the soap from his shower and the detergent he uses, which doesn't smell floral or anything. Just clean.

I squint at the screen. "Oh. That's right. I lived with Esther the last time I got fired."

"I can't believe there's been more than one time." He grimaces. "I'm sorry. That came out wrong. I mean that I'm sorry you had to deal with all this more than once."

I laugh but don't pick my head up from his shoulder. He seems not to mind, and this kind of touch feels nicer than the hug. Less vulnerable, but still ... nice. "Well, Ben Barber, I've been fired quite a few times in my long life."

He looks down at me, face serious. "That's their loss. They don't know what they're giving up. Fuckers."

"Ha! Fuckers." I lean forward as he types. "So,

you think if you just get the addresses right it'll sync up and ... holy shit! It says pending already!"

Ben grins. "Don't make me call my state representative to fast track this application. Because I absolutely will."

"I didn't even know you could do that."

He nods and closes the laptop, sliding it into his bag. "You can do it, too, Eila. That's what our elected officials are for. Partly."

"I'll keep that in mind." I straighten my hair and smile at him, not knowing what to say next. I think of his request to kiss me. I think about how I might respond differently if he asked today.

He seems to gather himself emotionally and I feel the change in his demeanor as he stands and crumples the napkins I scattered around the table. "Ready to head out? I can give you a ride if you're going home. I'm headed that way for a job..."

I smile and watch as he carefully sorts our stuff into compostable and garbage, neatly stacking our glassware in the bussing tub by the counter. "Thanks, Ben. I'm good."

He stands awkwardly by the door, scratching the back of his neck. I decide I want to try another hug, realizing I've been approaching this embrace with the same hesitation Ben brought to his rabies shots. I smile and open my arms, gesturing for a hug. Ben seems utterly delighted and relieved by this gesture and pulls me in for what I can only describe as a bear hug. I like it a lot this time, the firm wrap of his arms. I think about the fur on his stomach, feel the tickle of his shaggy hair against my forehead. "Thank you," I murmur into his shirt, giving him a sniff to tide me over the rest of the day.

"Any time, Eila." He releases me, face cracked in a huge smile. He waves and walks out the door. I grip the edge of the trash can, feeling a tiny bit like I might just swoon.

23

———

BEN

As I make my way through my day, rolling my eyes at messed up wiring and absolutely bananas attempts at drywall, it occurs to me that I don't want Eila to kiss me, necessarily. I want her to feel my desire. I want her to be so convinced of my support for her that she's overcome with the urge to mash her lips against mine.

Maybe there's not really a difference, but even I can tell that earning her trust will take work. I smile at the realization that the way my brain works actually lends itself to this situation: I can meticulously, step-by-step prove to Eila Storm that I support her projects and, by extension, her. Fully. Above and beyond.

When I get back to the office to drop off my paperwork, I swing through the Adopt a Lot office and grab a bunch of pamphlets for Eila. They have information on local companies testing solar-powered automated irrigation and access to grants for fencing. I think about the strangers hurling tires and garbage onto her lot in the past and preemptively fill out the top of the fence forms for her.

I know Eila has all the time in the world to monitor and water her plants right now, but eventually she will be back working, and I suspect she'll be really interested in the solar robot watering system.

I text her a selfie of me holding the pamphlets and then, thinking of how she pressed up close to me when we filled out forms at the coffee shop, ask if she will stop by my apartment to finish out some of this paperwork.

Not wanting to overwhelm her, I add:

Unless you're paperworked out. Totally understandable if you want to quit while you're ahead.

EILA STORM:

No, we're on a roll. Let's do it!

ME:

I will crank up my AC for you, Eila Storm.

I add an ice cube emoji for fun, making this the

first time in my life I've used an emoji or considered doing so to be fun.

EILA STORM:

[overheated emoji] Can't wait! See
you in 20.

I head home with a smile on my face and, after I walk Maurice, I treat both of us to Gershwin's "Walking the Dog" on the piano.

I lose myself to the jazzy music, winking at Maurice when he yips periodically as I play. By the time I get to the fast part, I'm immersed, letting the sounds carry me as I pour out all my energy into the keys.

24

EILA

I FEEL like I invaded Ben's privacy, caught him doing something deeply personal as I stand in his doorway watching him make love to his piano. There's really no other way to describe what's happening as I watch him sway in time to the music he creates, his hands lovingly stroking the keys.

He has his eyes shut and his face is so relaxed, so peaceful. I am transfixed. I realize with every passing second that music is a full-body experience for the performer, when it's done right. Every part of Ben is engaged in this song he's playing, from his taut back-muscles that move with his breath to the flexing of his legs as he does something to the pedals on the piano.

A tear sneaks down my cheek as I watch him, as I listen to him, as I *feel* the music flowing through me, too. This is just some dumb classical song I would have tuned out in music class in school, only now it's like the anthem to my life. The song is so emotional—sad and slow, angry and fast.

Why have I never appreciated this kind of thing before? The music picks up speed and, still staring, I see that Ben isn't even using music. He's got this entire song inside his head and his body just knows what to do with it all. He's like a flower unfolding in the sunshine.

Another tear slides onto my face, and I realize this kind of skill requires so much dedication, so much time. Ben is not a man who walks away from something. I see it, I sense it in my gut, and I feel something snap off and crumble inside me—something I've been carrying a long, long time.

Ben plays and plays and when he finally slows to a stop, he holds his hands above the keys for a few beats. As the final note dissipates, I take a shuddering breath, which he must hear because he spins around on the bench and stares at me.

Uncaring about consequences, I rush forward and plaster myself against him, diving onto his lap on the bench and straddling him, smearing topsoil all over his tidy clothes while I dig into his hair to bend his face up and kiss him.

Once my mouth collides with his, I can't stop. I inhale the tiny gasp he emits, and I squeeze him with my thighs and arms alike. Slowly, he takes stock of the situation and I feel his body work through stages of realization until he's kissing me too. Pressing his palms into my back. His fingers begin to move on me like I'm the keyboard and I groan, rocking myself against him.

He's hard now; I feel it through his khakis. I'm frantic, horny beyond belief, and I push him until his back hits the keys with a jarring, discordant sound. I don't let him respond, sliding my tongue into his mouth instead and stroking along his. I feel his heart racing against my chest where mine responds in time.

We kiss and I bash his body against the keys until the dog yips and brushes against my bare ankle. I pause and feel Ben smiling against my mouth. My eye meets his and he says, "hey."

I pull back, just a hair, to respond. "Hey."

His hands keep moving against my back, fluttering in a way I can just feel through the denim of my overalls. Why am I wearing such thick fabric? "I lost track of the time. How long have you been here?"

I shrug. "I'm here now."

He nods. "I can see that."

I drop a hand to his crotch. "I want to revise our agenda."

Ben draws in a gulp of air and his eyes fly wide,

as if I hadn't just spent the past five minutes with my tongue in his mouth. "Are you—"

"Don't ask me if I'm sure. I've never been more sure of anything, Ben Barber."

He stares at me, his dark eyes a deep sea of pupil with the tiniest ring of dark iris. And then he stands up with me on his lap like he regularly deadlifts a buck fifty. "The piano hurts my back," he growls, striding down his short hallway toward a bedroom I'm sure is as sparse as the rest of his apartment. As I flop onto the bed on my back, I figure this room has everything I need.

Ben's eyes are wild, nearly frantic above me and his mouth opens and closes a few times before he says, "I want you so desperately, Eila. I feel like I have been wanting you for forever." The look in his eyes reveals that he means this, fully and completely. There is no question that I am his sole focus right now and damn if that doesn't turn me on even more.

"I'm here." I start wriggling out of my overalls and I still when his hand snakes out and expertly unhooks one of the shoulders like he's starting a new piece on the piano or something. Maintaining intense eye contact the entire time, he peels the overalls down my legs and tosses them across the room.

He drops a warm palm to my thigh, and I stare

at it, feeling the weight of this touch through every nerve in my body. "Eila."

"Ben."

"I need to make you feel good. Will you tell me what you like?"

I stare at him. No man has asked me this before. Sex has always been frenzied. Sometimes I come if I'm on top. Sometimes the guy will fiddle around with my clit a few times while he pumps on top of me and then it's over.

Ben's thumb begins to lightly stroke my inner thigh while his fingers remain splayed across my leg, and I had no idea this was such a sensitive part of my body. I watch as he waits for me to answer him. "Mm. That," I manage to get out. "That feels good."

"Your eyes flutter when I touch you that way," he says, like he's taking notes. God, he is definitely taking mental notes. He arches a brow and kneels on the bed between my leg, dropping his other hand to my other thigh. "And then?"

I shrug and his expression darkens. I think of his hands on the piano keys, the stroking and pressing. "Touch my nipples," I spit out and he nods, pleased to have some direction.

I start to lift off my tank and see that my nips are already hard inside my bra. I regret not wearing lacy under things, but I had no idea I'd be spread out on

Ben's bed in my cotton briefs and ratty sports bra. It's been so hot outside...but then I stop being able to think coherently when he pinches my nipples through the stretchy fabric of the bra.

I reach a tentative hand up to his shoulder, so firm inside his polo shirt. I want to tell him to strip so I can see him, too, but I lose my ability to speak when he peels the bra up over my boobs and licks.

25

BEN

SHE TASTES INCREDIBLE. I gaze down at my hand, rough against the soft skin of Eila's breast, amazed that I've actually been invited to touch her this way. I lick her nipple again, relishing the sounds she makes, watching as she squirms on my bed. "Good?" I catch her eyes, hooded and dark. She nods and I keep going, massaging the small, firm curves with both hands as I lick. My blood pulses in my groin in response to the sounds Eila makes. Her skin tastes salty and perfect.

Inspired, I blow on one of the nipples and enjoy the delightful sound Eila releases as her hips shoot up from the bed, crashing into my erection like the final note of that Gershwin piece.

I trail a hand along her stomach, slowly stroking as I make my way toward her hip. "It seems like you're looking for pressure … here." I press my palm to her panties, causing her to groan.

"Ben!" My name is a gasp in her throat and her hands knead the sheets. "Holy shit, please. Touch me." Her voice is gravely, desperate. I've brought her to this state, and I throb with the pleasure of knowing that. Eila brings one palm to her nipple as I cup her sex, observing how much she likes that stimulation. I adjust my weight so I can rub her nipple and her clit. As soon as I locate her pleasure center, that is.

Lazily circling her nipple, I let my other hand slide into her underwear. Eila growls and shoves the cotton down her legs, kicking them across the room. And then she's naked. On my bed. She has what the guys at work call a farmer's tan, which I suppose is accurate. From her mid-thighs to her toes and collar to fingertips, Eila's skin is a dark olive.

But her stomach glows nearly white against my dark sheets. Eila spreads her legs, whimpering, and I see pink folds glistening beneath her dark curls. I reach for her damp heat and nod, feeling and hearing the effect this contact has. "This is so slow. God, I can't stand it," she whimpers. "You have to touch me, Ben."

I frown and lick her nipple again. "I really feel like I need to study you more carefully before I go barging in."

Eila pushes up on her elbows and grabs my face. "You are not comparing me to one of your inspection jobs, Ben Barber. Now make me come." I arch a brow and she bites her lip. "Please."

Feeling calmer than I would have expected at a time like this, I lean in and kiss her again. "Oh fuck, that feels amazing," she wails. I let my tongue slide into her mouth, tasting the savory warmth of her. While we kiss, I give her a bit of what she asked for, pressing a fingertip along her seam, exploring until I feel the stem of her clitoris.

She bites my lip, solidifying my guess. "How do you like to be touched?"

Eila blinks at me. "You're doing great."

I shake my head. "No, I mean ... firm? Light?"

I adjust the pressure as I ask, and she sucks in her breath. "All of it. Oh, fuck. Wait. That one. That oneeeeeee!" I nod, pressing firmly into her body, watching her face shift as the sensation flows through her.

I lean back, suddenly overcome with the need to see things up close. I make my way down her body, parting her thighs and touching her where I can see. The muscles of Eila's legs form a cage around my upper back and as she hauls me closer to her center, I can smell her arousal. Heavy and salty, tangy, and just perfect. I move closer and taste her, the thickness blooming across my tongue and I moan into

Eila's body as she digs her hands into my hair and clamps me in tight.

"Ben, holy shit. This is incredible. Wow. Wow!" Eila spews a litany of surprised sounds as I continue my exploration. I am amazed that I'm capable of taking her apart like this. I'm in awe of the way she just lets go to the feelings overtaking her body. The trust she is showing me right now practically shimmers in the room and I tingle in appreciation.

Eila's heels dig into my shoulders when I give her clit a long lick, so I keep at it until I feel her start to spasm around my fingers. Only when the screaming stops and her body stills do I disentangle myself and crawl back up the bed.

I'm on my back in a flash, a dark-haired pleasure goddess straddling me and yanking furiously at my belt and khakis. Eila's eyes are wide as she rips off my clothes and buries her hands in my chest hair. "Holy. Shit. Ben." She kisses my stomach and stares at my cock, which is impossibly hard. "I want to sit on this."

I stare at her, knowing that the second I'm inside her I am likely to explode. "You are incredible," I whisper, loving the feel of her fist around my length. Eila rubs a thumb over my tip, cooing, and I squeeze my entire body as I try not to come.

She explores my body with her other hand, looking drunk. I love that I helped her move into this space, made her feel this good. "Condoms?" She raises her brows hopefully and I wrack my brains for words.

"Bathroom," I choke out. "In the mirror."

Eila nods and pops off the bed. Before I can tell her I'll go get them, she's gone and back again, a strip of Trojans clutched in her fist. "Ha!" She rips one off and throws it at me. "Put it on. I want to watch."

I open the packet and comply. "You like watching this part?"

She nods. "I love how it looks when you touch yourself." A flush creeps up her cheeks at that admission as I wrap my hand around the base of my cock.

"You like this?" It sounds silly to be talking to her like this, but it never occurred to me that a woman might enjoy the sight of me fisting my junk.

"Oooh, Ben, it's so hot." She trails her hands along my thighs, staring. I stroke myself slowly as she watches, and I suck in a ragged breath. Thankfully, Eila grabs the condom and rips it open. "Put it on now, please." The second I do, Eila straddles me and lines herself up. I can't look away from the sight of her above me, her beautiful curves up close. Sinking down slowly, she moans, nearly drowning out my own sounds.

Fully seated, Eila leans forward and plants her

palms on my chest. I savor the feel of each connection point, but soon am overwhelmed by the hot glide of Eila wrapped around me. "Fuck, Ben." She looks down, staring at herself spread around my hardness. "I'm so full right now. Everything is so warm and hot and perfect."

All I can do is nod and gently roll my hips. I bring my palms to her backside, feeling her glorious curves as she moves on top of me. I swallow, nearly choking on the urge to just thrust up into her like a wild beast. "Eila," I sputter. "So close."

She nods. "Go on, Ben. Fuck me. Fuck me 'til you come. Oh! I feel you." I swell inside her, eyes squeezed shut, blasting off inside the last and only woman I ever want to do this with.

26

EILA

"WHAT CHANGED YOUR MIND?" Ben nuzzles my ear as he holds me close against him, naked under the covers while the frigidly powerful air conditioner cools the room.

"Hm?" It's hard to think after coming so hard, after staring into his intense eyes, seeing all the obvious affection there, directed at *me*. I just need to lie here, thrumming and buzzing and marinating.

Ben runs his palm along my side, his work-worn hand a little scruffy against my skin. I like it. "You told me I wasn't someone you'd just fuck and move on. And I have a hard time understanding people, so I'm hoping you'll tell me what changed your mind."

I roll over in his arms to face him, biting my lip. "This is hard for me."

"Mm I can be hard for you, Eila."

He chuckles and I swat at him. "I'm serious."

He kisses my nose. "I know. I apologize. Tell me."

"I saw you at the piano, totally lost to the music. And I thought about the work and dedication you must have put in to be able to do that, to create those sounds ... and the whole reason I came over here tonight was because you went out of your way to do something nice for me."

"Yes." He kisses my face like he's delighted he gets to do it.

I shrug. "I decided I could risk trusting you. A little."

"Just a little?" Ben's lips tip up in a smile and I realize he's relaxed right now. I don't know if I've ever seen him in this state. His limbs feel loose, his energy is calm. I reach for his hand, and he weaves our fingers together. I like it. I like everything about how I feel right now, about what we're doing.

"Tell me about the forms you got. The ones that led to this booty call." I smack his butt and he stiffens.

"Do we have to call it that?"

"What would you prefer? A merging of souls?" I laugh and the sound seems to delight him because, while he doesn't laugh, he does broaden his smile.

Eyes closed, Ben pulls me tight. "I got some paperwork for you to get grants for fencing and solar panels. Things for the hops lot since I know you don't have an income right now."

"Wow." I wriggle free and sit up against his headboard. Because of course he has a headboard like a real adult and not a mattress on wood pallets on the floor like me and Eden have. "There are grants for that stuff? That's incredible, Ben. Because you're right—it'll be months before I get any kind of income from the harvest."

He laces his fingers behind his head, one elbow resting on my naked thigh. "It's good to start out with your lot expenses separate from your regular income."

"What do you mean?" I trace my fingers through his hair.

"The hops harvest—you can get a separate account for that, and you'll know what to invest back into the lot, separate from your day job, so to speak."

I laugh. "Day job. That's funny."

He sits up, frowning. "Do you think you'll wind up working second shift? Or nights? Where all have you applied?"

I blink at him. "What do you mean? I haven't applied anywhere." A trickle of dread swirls at the base of my spine, creeping up along my ribs and chilling my neck. I can tell Ben is about to reveal something hurtful and I really don't think I can handle that after what I just shared with him.

"Eila." He places a palm on my thigh and turns toward me, gathering the sheets over his nakedness. "It sounds like you're saying you're planning for the hops project to be your sole source of income."

I blink at him again. My heart pounds forcefully in my chest and a lump forms in my throat. "I've been telling you that for weeks. This is what I want to do, Ben. I thought you were helping me."

He recoils, eyes flashing with something I can't identify. "How can you seriously believe that will be enough, Eila? You have 3,000 square feet of land. How much can you possibly grow there? You'd be one drenching rain away from an entire year without income."

I inch away from him on the bed, shaking. "I did all the calculations. You saw them. This will work." He frowns and shakes his head. My voice lowers to a whisper as I try to talk around the hairball growing in my windpipe. I know he's right, that one lot won't do it. But he's known this all along and I just assumed he was going to help me get there. Somehow. "I can expand, work with more lots..."

Ben stands and reaches for his pants. He sits on the bed with his back to me, tugging on clothes and talking. "Let's go get my laptop. We'll look up some numbers together, find you something you can do to supplement—"

I jump out of the bed. "I don't want to supplement anything. I've been working on *this.* Nobody has ever in my life supported one of my ideas." I yank my tank top on, leaving my bra wherever it might have landed. I search for my shorts. "I thought you believed in me."

I shake my head and walk toward the door, cramming my feet in my untied shoes. I want to vomit. I'm furious for letting myself trust Ben in this way, for believing that he was different from every other person in my life who just thinks I'm a fuckup. Maurice looks up at me from his little nest by the piano and I avert my eyes, unable to look even Ben's dog in the face right now.

"Eila, wait. Please don't leave like this. Let's talk."

I don't wait for the rest of his sentence. I slam the door behind me as I run down his steps and into my sister's van. Tears cloud my vision as I speed off into the night and make my way home.

27

BEN

"I screwed everything up. Again."

I sit on the couch in my therapist's office, twitching. My knee hammers like a piston and I tug at my shirt collar, feeling it strangle me despite opening the buttons on my polo for the first time ever. "I never meant to upset her," I spit out. "I was just pointing out logical facts."

Dr. Morgan nods and smiles. She leans forward a bit in her seat. "I know you didn't intend to hurt Eila's feelings. We've discussed how sometimes blunt statements of facts can feel insensitive to other people." I nod as she reminds me that I tend to see things in black and white terms with no blurred lines while Eila likely focuses more on emotions.

"I get all that. But what do I *do*? How do I fix this?"

"An apology is a good start, I bet," Dr. Morgan says. "But I wonder if explaining your reasoning to Eila would help? Provide some gentle context for what you said. An example might be, 'Eila, I'm sorry I came across so harshly. I want you to know I think your project is meaningful and I believe in your ability to succeed. My intention was to point out a challenge, not to hurt you.' Something like that will show her you care about her dreams, explain a bit about your thought processes."

I stare out the window. "I still don't understand how she thought this would be her sole source of income."

Dr. Morgan taps her notebook. "Do you need to understand how she came to think that? It sounds like she was looking for help making it happen ... not another person telling her that her ideas are too much."

I frown. "I'm not good at feelings or motivations or any of that."

"I understand." Dr. Morgan shrugs. "This is something many autistic adults struggle with. And it's why we're working together, right? Remember, you have a unique viewpoint. Use your strengths in logic to carefully choose your words. You can validate Eila's feelings while still being true to your perspective."

"Validating her feelings...I'm not sure I really understand what you mean." I furrow my brow so deeply I can see my own eyebrows.

Dr. Morgan nods again. "Gotcha. So. Given your relationship with your mother and sister, you haven't had many experiences feeling validated or accepted."

My leg stills and I clench my hands into fists. "No. Not really. Mom was always frustrated when I didn't react the way she expected me to." I run a hand through my hair. "She doesn't understand me."

Dr. Morgan smiles. "I theorize that Eila is feeling misunderstood, too. Validating her feelings means making an effort to recognize, and understand her emotional experience. So, when you tell her you understand her project means a great deal to her and ask her about why it's meaningful, it gives her space to explain her passion and share that with you."

"Even if her passion won't lead to the financial security she says she's looking for ..."

Another shrug from my therapist. "We have no way of knowing what will or will not happen. You've mentioned that you were helping her make plans, charts, datapoints..."

I sink into the couch and blow out a breath. I'm still not sure how last night was both the best night of my life and the worst. How in one moment I managed to convince Eila to trust me with her body and the next, I drove her from my apartment in tears. "I need her to understand that I'm on her side. That I want the best for her, for her to be happy."

Dr. Morgan smiles. "Relationships take skill and time. Don't worry if it feels awkward at first. The important thing is making the effort to understand Eila's emotions."

As per usual, I leave the session exhausted. I had no idea trying to understand myself and my interactions with others would feel so unsettling.

I dial Eila's number again and wince when the call goes right to voicemail. Before my brain can spiral into worst case scenarios, I send her a text asking her to at least let me know she made it home safely last night.

I want to text her so many things. I want to apologize for jumping to fix-it mode when it seems like she wasn't looking for my logic at the time.

Back at my office, I rifle through the remaining sites I have to visit today. I glance at a map of the city, the vacant lots seeming to shout at me in yellow on my computer screen. Eila has shown me the math and she's definitely done her homework on hops as a crop. But even if she took over 20 lots, she'd have to harvest within a three-day window—according to her own notes—and that would mean hiring staff and resting her entire year's income on this one event with more variables than I care to calculate.

Plus, what the hell will she do with herself the other 360 days each year?

No. That's not my business to worry about. If she wants to sit in her front yard and stare at the sky when she's not harvesting, then so be it.

There simply must be something out there that lets her take the time she'll need to tend this crop she values so highly while also providing a modicum of stability. Hasn't she told me how awful it's been growing up without any sort of safety net?

I close my eyes and click away from the map. I don't know how to bounce back from this.

28

EILA

Of course it's raining. Not only does the gray sky suck away any joy I might have found outdoors today, but it also sort of makes me unnecessary in the garden.

I try to silence the voice in my head shouting that I'm unnecessary pretty much everywhere. It's rough. I hear Eden leave the house and begrudgingly drag myself out of bed.

I water my shower plants and wander through the house with a spray bottle, misting all the herbs on the porch and the sweet potato vines I trained all along the front windows as an experiment in natural window treatments.

I'm stuck in between the memory of Ben worshiping my body and his shock that I thought I could actually make a career of hops farming on vacant lots. I spend about an hour spiraling about it before I decide I need my big sister. Esther will probably come at me with the same information as Ben, but it'll feel better coming from her. Hopefully she'll also know someone with advice.

I decide to walk to Esther's bar, despite the rain. I've got nice rain gear and am craving the time outdoors. I'm not used to being an indoor cat, as Esther sometimes calls Eva.

Bridges and Bitters isn't open yet, but I tap on the glass door until my sister looks up from her paperwork, frowns, and lets me in. "You look terrible."

"Nice to see you too, sis." I sink into a chair at the bar and flop onto the wood surface.

Esther sighs and tosses me a towel. "You're dripping on my floor, Eila. What brings you in?"

I drop the towel and rub it around with my shoe, mopping up the puddle I made around the chair. I take off my raincoat and hang it over the back of my chair and shake out my hair, feeling chilly in the cool air of my sister's workplace. "Ben and I had a fight."

Esther arches a brow and closes her notebook, reaching beneath the bar. I hear the sound of ice hitting a glass and I watch as my sister mixes me a drink. She slides the amber liquid across the bar without fanfare. "You've got about twenty minutes before my friends get here for lunch. Spill."

I sip the drink and smack my lips when the whiskey hits my tongue. Esther has blended it perfectly with whatever she used as a sweetener and, of course, bitters. "You made me an Old Fashioned? Like I'm some sort of elderly man?"

My sister crosses her arms, her tattoo flexing on her forearm as she gives me the stink eye. "Classy ladies also enjoy classic cocktails, Eila. Is it not delicious? Does it not inspire you to bare your soul to me?"

I roll my eyes. "He doesn't think the hops on lots can be my real job. He thought it was a side hustle."

Esther grips the edge of the bar, waiting for me to continue. I take another sip of my drink. "I just ... thought he was the one person who had faith in me and my ideas. I know it's a long shot."

My sister sighs. "Look, I've already asked you about your numbers and you didn't want to talk practicalities. Is that what you want today? I'm always happy to work through a business plan with you, Eila. You know that."

I squeeze my eyes shut. "The business plan depends a lot on forces beyond my control." I take a deep breath and meet my sister's gaze. "But I know I can push the buy local angle and I know I can sell. I know it, Esther. You know I'm good with plants."

Esther arches a brow. "But..."

I swirl the ice in my glass and stare at my lap.

"But best-case scenario I'd be, like, living on minimum wage."

Esther walks around the bar and pulls up the stool next to mine. She drapes an arm around my back and rests her chin on the top of my head. "Tell me why hops and why vacant lots. I mean, you could have planted up the entire ugly side of your house if you really wanted more space for a cash crop."

"My house is not ugly." I sniff into Esther's shirt, and she laughs. "The teal paint was on sale."

"For a reason." Esther plants a kiss on top of my head and releases me from this side hug. "Why hops?"

I release a deep breath and turn my palms face up. "In addition to being the secret to amazing beer ... I love that they don't take much to thrive. They twine onto other things, but they don't destroy like ivy does. They hardly need any soil, and they make something magical." I blow my hair out of my face. "Hops unlock the fermenting, boiling mush liquid and turn it into something beyond—something incredible. And vacant lots, I don't know."

Esther squints and I pop an ice cube into my mouth, crunching it with my teeth. I turn to face her. "The lots are abandoned ... they're left to their own devices without any guidance. They're overrun by weeds and invasive species taking advantage of them. Stripping their soil. Eroding the land. It really doesn't take much care to turn them around, help them thrive."

Esther is silent for a bit, and I see a tear form in the corner of her eye. "Of course you can see that, Eila. I had no idea, and I never thought about it that way." My sister wipes her face with her hands and shudders. "I tried my best to give all you girls the love I know you needed. But ... in the end, you really needed *parents*. And we never had that."

I nod. "I know that. You did great, Esther. I love you so much. I always knew you would do what you could."

She squeezes my hand. "Yeah, but honey, I am really seeing that you are freaking traumatized. And I think you need to find help working through all that so you can move on into your amazing future."

"Well. I was trying to do that. With my project. Like ... if I could save this one lot, it would feel like it made up for nobody looking after me. I know it's dumb."

Esther shakes her head. "It's not dumb. But it's also not a career path." We stare at each other for a long while. And damn her, Esther keeps my eye the whole time, like she knows I need to sit and stare at her until I accept that I've been a stubborn ass.

I'm on the verge of a good sob, about to ask Esther to give me a job washing glasses or something.

She puts a finger under my chin. "Do you want to stay for meatballs and do a career consult with the Foof ladies?"

My sister's friends call themselves Foof, for Fresh Out Of Fucks. They meet at her bar and rage about shit and, apparently, offer job consultations. "I feel weird doing that. They're your friends."

"Eila. This isn't high school. We can have friends in common." As she says the words, the door to the bar opens and I see Esther's friends Piper and Samantha duck in under their umbrellas. I'm surprised by the delight on their faces upon seeing me here, invading their friend-lunch. But both of them rush over to where Esther and I are sitting.

"Good thing I brought extra balls," Piper says, laughing at her juvenile joke as she sets a fragrant package on the end of the bar. My mouth waters as my sister digs out plates and forks. There's a gourmet meatball cafe down the road that I can never afford to enjoy. If the Foof ladies are offering classy meat, I don't have it in me to say no.

The door opens again, and Chloe Preston runs inside, carrying a box of books she gleefully plops on the end of the bar. "Fresh off the presses." She holds up one of the books and my eyes widen seeing the cover. Chloe writes steamy historical romance novels, and this one is evidently about a man who plows fields with no shirt on. "Eila, want an early review copy?" She slides me one of the books. I glance at my sister, who nods.

"Thank you. I've never read one of your books before."

Chloe grins. "Well, you're all grown up now and it's time you dove in." She pulls up a stool and reaches for a plate of meatballs. Soon we are all seated around the bar tasting the different boxes Piper brought.

And then my sister embarrasses the crap out of me by saying, "Eila needs help brainstorming job leads."

I whip my head to face her, about to tell her to please shut up, but Samantha claps her hands. "We always need good people at Vinea. What are you interested in doing?"

Esther gestures with her fork. "She has a certificate in horticulture. And she's obviously interested in something urban."

"Hmm." Samantha frowns. "Well, I can't really help with that. But if you ever consider a pivot to office work, I'm getting desperate."

Chloe swallows her food and grins. "Well. Now that you mention it, I saw something the other day when I was in Homewood Cemetery for research."

I frown at her. "Why were you researching in the cemetery?"

Chloe taps the book. "I do all kinds of historical

research for these babies. So anyway, I saw the cemetery is hiring a horticulturalist. Which I never thought of before, so I was reading the description, and they are looking for someone to manage the arboretum and gardens." She looks around the group. "Did you know someone wrote a book about that cemetery? It's like 200 acres and has 40 species of trees."

Samantha shakes her head and laughs. "Only you would know that, Chlo."

Piper holds up a finger. "I knew! I take fitness clients in there for walks. The hills are great cardio for my seniors."

I blink in surprise as my sister pulls a job listing up on her phone. "Is that the actual salary? Seriously?"

Esther nods and taps her screen. "And look at that. Full benefits." She grins. My hands shake as I scroll through the listing, astonished that there might be a way to grow in a new direction while still staying rooted in my hops plan. Esther smiles knowingly. "You could get yourself some really good therapy in exchange for fending off invasive species from the beech trees."

29

BEN

I keep making bad choices. I'm currently slumped in a booth at a brewery with Cash, too drunk to get myself home, and worried about Maurice.

My friend seems way too sober to have been matching me drink for drink, and he stares at me like he's waiting for me to say something. "What?"

Cash rolls his eyes and growls. "Have you been listening to me at all?"

I shake my head. At least I think I do. I got my final rabies shot today and took the afternoon off, too overwhelmed by the needle and having ruined things with Eila to even consider objectively inspecting anybody's property.

Cash snaps his fingers in front of my face. "I asked you the plan to win her back. What's your grand gesture?"

I squint at him. "I have no plan. I suck at this. I can't solve this problem."

Cash waves a hand. "This is a solvable problem. What's she like?"

I smile despite myself. "She's like sunshine. And hailstorms. And oregano."

Cash laughs and pulls my beer away from me, replacing it with a cup of water. "Dude. I meant what things does she enjoy. I should probably take you home..."

I'm about to tell him Eila likes plants and air conditioning when Piper appears at the door of the bar with ... no.

"Cash, you aren't going to believe who I had lunch with today." Piper tugs Eila Storm to the booth and nudges her to sit. She sits stiffly at the edge of the bench. Cash looks confused and Piper laughs. "Eila! Ben's Eila is Esther's Eila. I don't know why I didn't put it together before. I mean, there are a lot of Isla's with an I..."

Cash grins at my lady-friend. "So, you're Esther's sister. And Ben here has been wooing you."

I stare at Eila, watching as her cheeks turn pink. She swallows. "He has." She presses her lips together and the only sound comes from the din in the bar.

Piper slaps the table and turns to Cash. "We should probably go get Ruby."

He looks at his watch. "We've got another hour."

Piper leans forward toward Eila and me. "I'm so sorry he's so thick-headed." She turns to face Cash. "Take me home and massage my feet, and then we'll go get Ruby."

Cash scratches at his beard and I watch as he realizes his girlfriend wants to give Eila and me some privacy. They're gone before I can figure out what to say, so I just sip my water.

Eila sniffs. I stare at her. "God, you're beautiful," I blurt out. I reach for her face and remember that she's mad at me, so my hand just sort of hangs in the air for a bit.

Eila smiles. But not all the way. "I'm really sorry I snapped at you and ran out, Ben. It wasn't really about the hops."

"I love your hops idea, Eila. I think it's so unique."

She nods. "It is, isn't it? But, I yelled at you for caring instead of managing my own shit."

I shake my head. "I was letting logic get in the way of validating your emotions."

She sniffs. "What does that even mean?"

I sigh and sink deeper into the cushioned booth. "I hardly know. These are things I talk about in therapy now."

Eila leans back against the booth and turns her

head to face me. We slump together side by side and she says, "I need to get some of that. Therapy."

I nod. "It's hard work. But I think it helps."

She grins. "So, I think I found a lead on a real job. One with benefits and all."

I pat her hand. "You're one step closer to a rabies vaccine, then."

"Yeah." She snorts. "Want to help me with my application?"

"Are you kidding? I want to help you with everything, Eila. Except shopping for my dog. He does not require a wardrobe."

Eila reaches for my water glass and takes a swig. "We will have to agree to disagree about that, Ben Barber. Maurice would look fetching in a jaunty scarf."

She squeezes my hand and then, seeing an employee emerge from the service entrance of the brewery, pops out of her seat. I squint as Eila slides her hands into the pockets of her overalls, biting her lip and talking to the man in rubber boots.

I smile when the man does, extending his hand for a shake, which Eila accepts before making her way back over to the table. I like that I have enough context to guess why she's talking to that guy.

Eila shrugs and says, "He's interested in seeing some paperwork about my hop lot." Overwhelmed with pleasure and desire, I lean across and kiss her cheek, resting my head on her shoulder.

Eila wanted to walk to the library to work on her job application, but I remind her that I have a laptop along with excellent air conditioning. She agrees to soberly drive my car home and help me get Maurice situated in exchange for whatever help she thinks I can offer her on the cemetery job application.

I watch from my kitchen window in lustful awe as she holds an umbrella over my dog while he pees on a trash can in the alley. The whole thing is weird and wonderful. When the two of them come inside, I greet them with treats: dog biscuits for Maurice and a glass of nearly frozen water for Eila, who sinks onto my piano bench with a sigh as she cradles the cold cup to her chest.

"How on earth did you find a plant job at a cemetery," I ask, typing in the password to my laptop and, embarrassingly, hiccupping.

She shakes her head. "I didn't. My sister's friends knew about it. Cemetery horticulture is a whole thing. Like ... a whole thing." She gestures for the laptop and clicks around. I lean toward her from the chair as she balances the computer on my covered keyboard. She points at the monitor.

"I won't even be dealing with graves. I'd be literally designing the landscaping, tending the trees, fighting back the knotweed." Eila claps her hands. "I already want to ask them if they've considered bringing in goats rather than using pesticides. And what if they let me install some bee boxes? I could get my whole family involved. The job listing says that as a designated arboretum they have to provide some community education..."

I reach a hand out to rub a thumb on Eila's cheek. I can't help it. And I inhale sharply when she rests her face against my hand, like she enjoys this touch. "Eila, it sounds perfect for you. All plants and no public."

The grin on her face lights up my entire room and I forget it's cloudy today. She waggles her eyebrows. "Would it be in poor taste if I asked about growing a hops garden in the cemetery?"

I spit out a laugh. "Maybe save that ask for after you're hired."

She scoots closer to me, and I drag the chair a bit closer to the piano bench, vowing to get actual furniture as soon as I'm sober enough to order some online. Eila clicks around on the online job application, seeming to forget that she asked for help. I watch her type, listening to her talk to herself as she does so, glad for the opportunity to just be close to her. She doesn't struggle with any of the questions and only pauses to tap her lip with her finger as she seems to calculate dates.

With a small gasp, she says, "That's the whole thing. Should I wait to send it?" She looks at me and I shake my head.

"Do it. You got this. You are uniquely qualified."

Eila squeezes her eyes shut and clicks submit. Then she lets out a roar. "Oh my god, I can't believe I did that. What if they don't call?"

"They will."

She turns to face me as I gently close the laptop and move it beside me on the chair. "But what if they don't?"

I reach for her hand and squeeze. "Then we'll find another job and I'll help you apply for it."

She gives me a little push. "Yeah, like you helped so much with this one."

I laugh. "Look. I provided excellent atmosphere for peak concentration."

Eila nods. "That's true." She takes a deep breath and smooths out her hair. "Will you play a song for me?"

My eyes widen. "Of course." Even fall-down drunk, I could play the piano. And I'm well on my way to sober at this point. Eila slides over on the bench and I join her on it, not even caring that she'll be in the way of the lower keys. I might just choose a song with a lot of low notes, so I have the excuse to lean against her while I play them.

Instead, I aim for an Irish song about gardens in honor of Eila's new endeavor. She watches intently as I pluck through the melody, swaying a bit with the upbeat song. When I play the last note, I let my fingers hover above the keys, so the final chord echoes in the room. As soon as the sound breaks, Eila squeaks and throws her arms around me. She presses her mouth to mine, kissing me softly, tentatively.

I turn to draw her in closer and return the kiss, but I don't deepen it. Not now. Instead, I pull her in tight in another hug. I hold her for a long time, until I feel her relax into my chest. "This isn't just a fling for me, Eila," I whisper into her hair.

I feel her nod against me. "I know that."

I inhale a shaky breath and reach for the confidence I feel when I'm playing music, for how I felt making love to her the other night. Because that's where my head and heart are right now. "I'm falling for you, Eila." It feels inadequate to say that, because the truth is I fell for her the minute I saw her.

"Ben." She pulls back and meets my eye, a smile on her face. "Me, too."

30

EILA

SIX WEEKS LATER

BEN NIBBLES my shoulder from behind me in his bed. "What are you doing?"

"Shh." I need to concentrate as I type an email on my phone. I read aloud as I clack out the words. "'Just a reminder that I have PTO today and Friday. If it does not rain, I will swing by before dark to make sure the sprinkler system is targeting the flower beds by the entrance gate. Thank you again for being' ... what word should I say here?"

I roll over to face Ben, who lies on his side, shirtless and smiling. I love sleeping over at his house, and not just because he has air conditioning. It's lovely to wake up with him and Maurice, drinking coffee and preparing for our days at work. He always falls asleep with an arm wound tightly around me, and I always love the possessive safety of that contact.

"Flexible," Ben says. "Thank them for being flexible with your schedule and then kiss me properly."

I nod and finish the email, stretching and smiling at him. I rub my fingers along his lips, enjoying the feel of him here. "Today's the day."

"I'm still waiting for my kiss."

"It feels surreal. The harvest and the kissing and all of it."

The past six weeks have been like a fairytale. The cemetery called me in to interview the day after I applied and I was able to start immediately. Which meant within a week, I had an honest to goodness salary, something called a 401k plan, and a boyfriend to hold my hand each time I freaked out about any of it.

Ben rolls on top of me, supporting his weight on his forearms. His hair tickles my forehead as he leans close. "I promise, I'm real."

I lift my face to meet his mouth, and he kisses me softly, tenderly. He's so … steadfast. So sure of his feelings for me. Each day that I get to enjoy that support and affection brings me closer to being sure of him as well.

Ben makes a low sound in his chest and then sinks onto my shoulder, giving me most of his weight. I love the pressure of it, the strong security of him physically and emotionally. "I can't believe you took off work to help me."

He twists in my arms, meeting my eye. "Why? I wouldn't miss it."

I bite my lip. I started therapy as soon as my health insurance kicked in. Esther's friend Sam hooked me up with an amazing female therapist, and I've been going every week for a month. The sessions leave me raw, like a frayed wire. But I'm learning how to talk about my feelings. "I'm not used to people supporting me, seeing things through." He opens his mouth and I touch his lips with my fingertips. "And you've done so much to show me you're here for me. I see you. I'm just saying ... it's new still."

He kisses my shoulder again. He knows how new all of this is, from preventative healthcare to a regular paycheck ... not to mention having a boyfriend. "Should we get going?"

I smile and nod, hopping out of bed. Ben made room in his closet for my collection of overalls, and while I love the look of them barely clinging to hangers next to his tidy polo shirts, I can tell the situation isn't sustainable for my boyfriend. Soon, I'll have enough cash flow to buy myself a chest of drawers to keep here, to make things more organized.

I tug on a tank top and cut-off overalls with a

pair of sturdy boots and a huge hat, since Ben and I will be in the sun the entire day picking hops by hand. He dresses quickly as I make my way to the bathroom to deal with my hair.

I hear the microwave beep in the kitchen, and I round the corner as he hands me one of the egg sandwiches we made in bulk and froze together last Sunday.

It seems boring to enjoy mundane things like food prep, but there's something so soothing about making an assembly line and carrying out a task with Ben's help. I spend more time here than at my house these days, but even when we are at my place, he helps me with laundry and dusting and all the normal things couples do on television. It all just feels so stable, and that gives me a bigger thrill than showering with my spider plants.

There was a time when even a whiff of stability made me uncomfortable. But that was before Ben. He's just relentlessly *there* for me. For Maurice. For my ideas. I suck in a happy breath and chew my healthy breakfast.

Ben carries Maurice to the car, and we drive to Garfield, where I have all my supplies set up and ready to go—labeled bins for the cones, a gentle rinsing station to knock off any debris.

Ben looks at me expectantly as I reach up to pluck the first of my precious plants. I wait, almost surprised nobody comes by to yell or shoo me away. But this is my project, and I am officially sanctioned to be here, harvesting these amazingly fragrant plants.

"Do it," Ben chants. "Pick it." Maurice yaps in agreement.

With a grin, I yank down the furry cone and drop it into the bin. Ben cheers and I join him with a loud whoop. And then we get down to business, picking in earnest.

By the time we break for lunch, I estimate Ben and I have hundreds of pounds of product loaded into the back of Eden's van.

Midway through the afternoon, Eden surprises me by dropping by the lot to help with the harvest. She says she's in between honey harvests, but I suspect something else is going on when Eliza also "drops by" on her way to check on one of her goat crews. I stand with my hands on my hips, shaking my head when Eva and Esther stride into the lot with spare sunscreen and a jug of iced tea.

"What are you all *doing* here? Don't you have shit to do?"

Esther hands me a glass of tea. "We thought we'd lend a hand. Smell this aroma you're always yakking about." She grins and gestures toward the remaining empty buckets. "Tell me what to do."

I should tease her about getting to boss her

around for once, but I'm too overwhelmed and I cough, the words stuck behind a lump in my throat. Ben demonstrates how to pinch the cones from the bines and with six of us working, we have the entire lot done and dusted in a matter of hours.

I stare at the utility van, stuffed to the brim with food grade bins of a crop I spliced and nurtured. One thousand pounds worth of hard work and support from the people currently jockeying to hug me in the golden sunset. I stop trying to hold back the tears and just let them streak through the green-gold dust on my cheeks.

Ben is at my side in a heartbeat, tipping my chin up so I meet his worried gaze. "Are you okay, Eila?"

I shake my head no, because okay is the wrong word for how I feel right now. "I'm ..." I flap my hands around and Ben nods, waiting patiently for me to continue. I clutch at my heart. "I'm supported."

"Yes, definitely." His smile is warm and he's back lit by the orange and purple clouds.

"That's a new sensation for me," I wail as Ben continues to nod. I feel the impact of the work I've done in therapy coming at me like a burst of wind, blowing away lingering self doubt. Today was a huge fucking day for me, and the people I trusted with that information came through. I cry in relief until I laugh, and then I'm just sort of making hysterical sounds as Ben rubs my back and my sisters make themselves scarce.

Eden climbs over the fence into our yard, checking on her hives. I hear her whispering softly to them that she hopes they've appreciated the new plants next door. I let her words distract me for a moment, thinking about how the hops might influence the flavor of her next batch of honey, but I don't have the energy to tell her that right now.

Ben's voice appears by my ear, his breath warm on my skin but not in a way that makes me sweaty. "You know everyone is here with you because we all love you, right? You know that I love you?"

I stiffen. Ben and I haven't used that word yet. But he's right. Of course he is. I knew it months ago when he asked to woo me and I realize I know it down to the soles of my garden boots. "I ... do know you love me, Ben." He presses a kiss to my temple and smiles at me, like he wants me to say it back but can wait for an eternity while I get myself ready.

Except ... I don't want to wait to be ready. I don't need to worry that Ben will slink off in the night when a better opportunity comes knocking. He is here, with me, at my worst and today, at my best. And I love that about him.

I gasp, realizing, and then I blurt, "I love you, too, Ben."

His smile could melt honeycomb and the arms

that pull me tight feel stronger than the clingiest plant vines I've ever tended. His lips press into my hair, his hands on my arms, tugging me close like he's trying to splice me into his own body. "I love you," he whispers again.

I don't know how long he holds me in the middle of the once-vacant lot we transformed together. Long enough that my tears dry and Maurice starts to lick my legs. With a final kiss on my cheek, Ben releases me and crouches to make sure Maurice has water.

I wipe at my face and turn toward my scattered family. "You guys coming along to the bar to make the drop?"

Eliza glances at the sky. "Nah. I gotta check on the girls. Eva, you want a ride or you going with Esther?"

My youngest sister shrugs. "I could feed a goat."

"You're not feeding them. We need them to eat the weeds."

"Whatever. Pet them. Visit. Let's go already." They climb into Eliza's truck and rumble away.

Esther offers me a salute. "I'm going to go shower and make sure Tilly has a handle on things at the bar. You'll let me know when the brewery has a keg ready for me?"

I wave her off, grinning. I turn to Ben. "It's just you, Maurice, and me making the delivery, I guess."

He nods and we climb into my sister's van to make the short trip to the brewery in the east end, near his friend Cash's house.

They agreed to buy the entire crop for a wet-hop IPA they plan to name Eye of the Storm.

I leave the delivery entrance a few thousand dollars richer and happier than I can ever remember feeling. Ben leans against the van, waiting for me outside. He snaps a picture of me with his phone and I glance down, confused why he'd want to document my sweaty mess.

"This is the face of a triumphant woman," he says, smiling at the phone. "Look at you, successful urban farmer." I lean against him and look at the picture, trying to see what he sees. And ... he's right. Despite the leaves in my hair and the dirt streaking my arms, I'm glowing. There's no other way to describe the look of satisfaction and pride shaping my face. "What's next, Eila?" He raises his brows.

I bite my lip and wiggle my own brows at him. "Next, I'd like to defile your shower."

His jaw drops and I giggle as I hop behind the driver's seat of Eden's van. I drive faster than I ought to back to his house, where he hurriedly serves Maurice his dinner while I strip in Ben's living room. My shirt lands on the arm of the new sofa Ben ordered, my socks hitting the new coffee table.

By the time I peel off my undies, Ben is sliding

across the floor on his knees, colliding with my body and palming my boobs with a growl. "How do you manage to look sexy *and* like you've just escaped an avalanche?"

I shrug and moan as he licks my nipples. Ben has shown me—repeatedly and thoroughly—that he excels at gentle lovemaking. He can strum my body like I'm his keyboard, but I'm feeling like something a little different today.

"Ben." I tug on his hair to pull his dark head back from where he's doing excellent things to my nipples.

"Mm?" He can't seem to remove his hands from my belly, thumbs tracing up and down my sides and sending shivers of delight through my spine.

I summon my remaining strength and shove him backwards, straddling him as I rip off his clothes in a frenzy. "I want to be wild with you," I growl. His eyes widen as I tug his belt free from his cargo shorts. Inspired, I tug off his shirt and lift his arms above his head. "I'm going to tie your hands to the piano bench," I declare, eliciting a groan from the man who works so hard to earn my trust.

I see every ounce of that reflected back to me as he lets me loop the belt around his wrists and tie a loose knot around the leg of the bench. He's always so tactile and I can tell this act of restraining his hands is a huge demonstration of his trust for me.

I'm electrified by the intimacy of this, of the power I hold right now. I nod at my shoddy restraint work and lick my lips as I drag my hands down Ben's toned, hairy torso. He moans, my name in his mouth, and I feel incredibly powerful as I explore this body I already know so well.

"Oh shit, Eila. What are you doing to me?" I slide my center along his body, feeling the wet drag of my folds against his skin. I reach for his throbbing length and kiss the tip, holding his stiff cock in my fist.

"Today's one week since I got the IUD," I tell him, rubbing his pre-cum with my finger and enjoying the way he wriggles beneath me. "Are you cool if we raw-dog it?"

"Anything, Eila." I lean down and kiss the silky tip of his length. He nearly chokes. "Fuck, fuck, *fuck* I want to touch you so much."

"Hmm," I smile at him, really loving the way he's surrendering himself, giving me all the power right now. I love how much he trusts me to understand his sensitivities, to make this feel good for him, too. "How about if you just watch me take you bare?"

I hover above him, lining myself up. Our eyes lock as I slide down his body, the velvet steel filling me in a hot rush that takes my breath away. "Eila," he whimpers. "Look at us."

We both stare as I spread around him, placing

my hands on his chest for balance as I find a rhythm that feels good. This is the sexiest thing I've ever done, and I want to savor it as much as I want to tear his hands free and fuck him frantically as he digs his fingers into my back.

I opt for the latter, knocking the belt loose from the piano bench and sighing when Ben's hands find purchase against my hips. Both of us grunt and growl as I move and the angle is so perfect, the pressure so right that he doesn't even need to touch me before I'm throbbing and pulsing around him.

"I want to feel you inside me all the time," I mutter. "Please, Ben. Let me feel you come."

His eyes flash and an anguished moan tears from his throat as he stiffens. He swells even larger inside me, and I throw my head back, coming in a massive wave as I feel the heat of his release flooding me.

"I love you, Eila. I love you so damn much."

I collapse forward onto his chest, sinking into the afterglow, enjoying the intensity I once cowered away from. "I love you, too, Ben."

31

BEN

TWO WEEKS LATER

"I just don't know about this, Ben. Isn't it weird? A party in a cemetery?" Mom frowns, clutching her purse to her chest on her porch.

I shrug. "Sure. It's weird. But it would mean a lot to me if you came and support my girlfriend."

Mom seems to gnaw on the inside of her cheek and then smiles. "I do want to meet your girlfriend. I just wish she didn't work in a *cemetery*." Mom whispers this last word like it's a secret the neighbors will disapprove of. Maybe they will. But I don't care what the neighbors think of my Eila. I'm proud of her, and she's mine.

I drive Mom to the cemetery, where Eila and the other staff members have created an open-house event to showcase the historic space. There are a lot of celebrities buried here, as well as some sculpture work by famous artists. And of course, some incredible landscaping by the best horticulturist in the entire world. If you ask me.

I park near the entrance, happy to see the number of cars who turned up. As Mom climbs out, I pop in the ear loops I bought for these sorts of public events with crowds and their associated noises. Mom frowns at the white loops and I explain, "these filter out a lot of the background noise. It makes it easier for me to concentrate on what specific people are saying."

"I see." She nods, like she doesn't quite, but I do know she's trying. A few weeks ago, I told her I'm autistic and shared some of what I'm working on with Dr. Morgan. Mom smiles and taps her chest. "You seem different, Ben."

I shrug. "I'm the same. I just have different strategies now and I know more about how to stay comfortable."

Mom looks like she's about to say something, but Eila charges up to us from the closest flower bed. "Is this her? Are you Mrs. Barber?" She throws her arms around my mom, who stiffens. Eila draws back. "Sorry. Are you not a hugger? I've been working on being more affectionate, but I guess not everyone appreciates that. I'm just so excited to meet Ben's mom!"

I slip an arm around her shoulders. "Eila Storm, Wendy Barber. Mom, this is my Eila."

Mom tears up and pulls Eila away from me, giving her a face pat and a loud cheek kiss, like she used to give me until a few weeks ago I explained that I like to be touched more firmly. Mom grips my shoulders and squeezes and I rest my cheek on the top of her head. Sniffing, Mom pulls back. "Now tell me more about this event."

Eila grins and gestures for us to follow her down the path. By the willow tree, she's set up a small stage and sound system, and our mutual acquaintance Chloe Preston, aka novelist Chloe Petals, is about to start a presentation about the historical research she conducts to write her steamy romances.

All the Storm sisters are present, along with Esther's husband and a large group of women wearing pins declaring they are Fresh Out Of Fucks. Piper, with Cash in tow, hands Eila one of the pins, and my lady joyfully attaches it to the strap of the new overalls she bought for this event—her one foray with the public in her official capacity at work.

After Chloe's bit, Eila's sister Eliza guides a group through the perimeter pathways, talking about the ways her goats represent a sustainable approach to contain invasive species that might otherwise destroy the landscape and the grave markers.

The event I'm really looking forward to is Eila's spotlight, when her boss introduces her as a spectacularly gifted horticulturist and hands Eila the microphone. I bite back a whoop as Eila grins at the crowd. "Thank you all so much for venturing out here today. I'm thrilled to help tend this magnificent landscape, which is still thriving today after 200 years—simply because 100% of the plants you see here are native to this area." Eila gestures around the vibrant wildflowers, still colorful and fresh in early September. "Look at the beautiful blooms, at how easily maintained this space is. With 200 acres and 9 miles of pathways, this cemetery is committed to right-sized effort for maximum visual impact. But we're also protecting an incredible biome." Eila talks about the scientists observing frog populations and migrating birds who find rest in the cemetery, above ground.

I love to watch her talk, so confident, so happy. She's still wild and unpredictable. She's still often crass and stubborn. But today she's comfortable and proud of what she's been able to achieve. She continues talking, saying, "I say these beds require limited care—not neglect. With the right amount of attention and direction, even the scrawniest vines can flourish."

She meets my eye and I blow her a kiss, glad I have a reason to stare at her now. I hover near the back of the gathering. I am grateful Eila has a lot of people here to join her love of noise and celebration. Grateful we've got a mini-keg of Eye of the Storm on ice at my house, which I plan to share with her from the quiet comfort of my sofa.

Eila keeps trying to convince me this drink would make an ideal shower beer, but she's filled my shower with plants, and I can't handle the feel of the leaves against my skin when there are two of us in the shower stall. So, we're going to compromise.

I drop Mom off at home with a promise to bring Eila around for dinner sometime soon, and I swing back to the cemetery, where the crowds have dissipated, the silence has returned. I find Eila at the edge of the pond, running her hands along a row of cattails.

"You ready to go?" I reach for her hair, always filled with fluff and particles from the plants with which she surrounds herself. She nods and wraps her fingers through mine, strong tendrils that bind us together—an unlikely pairing spliced into something powerful.

"Take me home, Ben Barber." She kisses my cheek, and we walk toward my car, arm in arm.

EPILOGUE: EDEN

My sisters are all so incredible. Eila's work event managed to showcase Eva's social media marketing skills and Eliza's goats and, of course, Eila's own amazing plant skills. I wish she'd have made a push to let me set up some beehives here, but this job is still pretty new for her. I get it.

I glance at my work phone out of habit. Nothing new. I usually get a lot of calls this time of year because bees tend to swarm into people's yards ... or houses ... or machinery.

I never meant to become a beekeeper. It's not like how Esther opened a bar on purpose and Eila was always going to be a professional plant lady.

I happened to be in the right place one day when someone found bees in their garage and, well, I just knew what to do. Now, here I am, selling honey and beeswax salves and, when I'm really lucky, getting paid to remove bees from other people's property.

But today is about Eila. I'm happy for her and Ben, I swear. Even though I can tell my sister is going to move out and then I'll be totally stuck with rent. Sure, I could move someplace smaller and probably afford to live alone. But it's not just me.

I've got five colonies of bees in the back yard, and that doesn't even include the spare boxes I've started storing on Eila's lot where she grows hops.

I smile and clap as my sister proudly details the native plants all throughout the cemetery. Who would have thought these old cemeteries were so carefully planned out? There's a flipping arboretum in here, and I just know those fruit trees would really benefit from a nice, active colony of honeybees. Oh well.

Eila catches my eye, hands in her pockets, and I wave at her from my place front and center of the little crowd consisting of all our sisters, their friends, and quite a few strangers just here for the vibes. Should I have brought business cards? Is that slimy, to promote my work at my sister's shindig?

Before I can decide, my work phone actually rings in my pocket. I back away from the group, hoping I'm not distracting my sister from her talk, and answer the phone without looking at the number. "Storm Swarm, this is Eden."

The caller coughs. And then I hear a voice I'd rather forget. "Eden? Hey. I've got a problem."

I pull the phone away from my face and stare at it. Of course I don't have his number entered into my contacts. This is my work phone. In my personal phone, I listed him as ACTUAL SATAN.

"Eden? Are you there?" His voice sounds tinny, far away. I take a few breaths and look around me, trying to decide if, I don't know, someone is pranking me. Somehow.

"Nate?" I hate the way his name feels in my mouth, my tongue heavy with uncertainty. This guy screwed me over last year. Big time.

"Yeah. It's me. I was hoping—"

"If you're calling to report more diseases, I assure you I've had all the tests. You can go jump in a river now, goodbye."

"Eden, wait!" His voice is just desperate enough to halt my thumb before I press the red button to end the call. "I'm calling about a professional issue, I swear."

I frown. Today is Saturday and it's late afternoon. Why is he working right now? Sounds fishy. "You have 90 seconds."

He sighs. "I'm flipping a house over in Point Breeze."

"So?" I look over my shoulder, realizing he's less than a mile away from me at the moment.

"Well. Um. The attic is full of bees."

My brows shoot up. "Oh yeah?"

"God, Eden, there must be a million of them. An actual million bees inside the walls."

I laugh. "There are probably two million if it's one of those big mansions."

I listen to him exhale, trying not to remember the sound and feel of him breathing near my ear while his hands roamed my body. "So, can you help me get rid of them? None of my guys will agree to work with all that going on."

I look at my sister, standing up on a rock and gesturing as she proudly describes responsible weed control here in the cemetery. I think again about the rent and the upcoming winter slow season. "It'll cost you," I hiss at Nate, before I spit out a fee double my usual rate to remove bees from a residential property.

"Fine. Whatever. How soon can you be here?"

Shocked, I mutter, "My stuff is in my van. Give me five minutes."

Nate texts me an address and I catch my sister Esther's eye at the back of the crowd. I point at my phone and mouth "work call."

She waves me off with a smile and I head off into

the literal sunset to rescue my ex from a swarm of bees.

Thank you for reading Ben and Eila's story! Eden's book, The Burgh and the Bees, is next in the Planted and Plowed series.

Want a glimpse into Ben and Eila's happily ever after? My newsletter subscribers get a bonus scene! Visit LaineyDavis.com to subscribe and see if Eila can help Ben shave before work.

AUTHOR'S NOTE

I was supposed to write this book a year earlier than I did. I got totally consumed by a news event and had to write an emergency book to process all that information.

I feel like Ben would find himself in a similar situation: utterly overcome by something or someone.

I've mentioned in the past that I live with neurodiverse people. I write a lot of neurodiverse characters on purpose because I want everyone to know those folks can and do find a happily ever after. But I'm learning I also write a lot of neurodiverse characters by accident.

For each of my books, I hire authenticity readers who share an identity aspect with one of my protagonists. I reached out to Autistic readers to help me create Ben's character and make sure he felt authentic. They overwhelmingly let me know that actually, Eila seems pretty neurodiverse, too.

That wasn't intentional! But of course as soon as they said that, I saw it clear as day. Ultimately, I did not adjust the plot to address that aspect of Eila's identity. During the scope of this story, she's focused on her career and her ability to trust people. Perhaps in the future I will revisit Eila and take her on a journey toward a diagnosis. For now, that's all just bonus information I now know about her character.

I am indebted to my early readers Karen Grey, Sara Whitney, Elizabeth Perry, and Nicky Lewis for their input. My authenticity readers Amy and Shea offered incredible feedback about Ben and the book overall.

And of course, I'm thankful to my readers who keep coming back for more. These books are for you!

ALSO BY LAINEY DAVIS

Bridges and Bitters series

Fireball: An Enemies to Lovers Romance (Sam and AJ)

Liquid Courage: A Marriage in Crisis Romance (Chloe and Teddy)

Speed Rail: A Single Dad Romance (Piper and Cash)

Last Call: A Marriage of Convenience Romance (Esther and Koa)

Planted and Plowed series

Against the Grain (Eila and Ben)

The Burgh and the Bees (Eden and Nate)

Yule Be Sorry (Eliza and ???)

Sappy Go Lucky (Eva and Asher)

Farm 2 Forking series

Since You've Bean Gone (Ethan and Lia)

Butter You Up (by Liz Alden)

For Fork's Sake (by Karen Grey)

Bringing Home the Bacon (by Erin Mallon)

A Fork in the Road (by Ember Leigh)

Binge the following series in eBook, paperback, or audio!

Brady Family Series

Foundation: A Grouchy Geek Romance (Zack and Nicole)

Suspension: An Opposites Attract Romance (Liam and Maddie)

Inspection: A Silver Fox Romance (Kellen and Elizabeth)

Vibration: An Accidental Roommates Romance (Cal and Logan)

Current: A Secret Baby Romance (Orla and Walt)

Restoration: A Silver Fox Redemption Romance (Mick and Celeste)

Oak Creek Series

The Nerd and the Neighbor (Hunter and Abigail)

The Botanist and the Billionaire (Diana and Asa)

The Midwife and the Money (Archer and Opal)

The Planner and the Player (Fletcher and Thistle)

Stag Brothers Series

Sweet Distraction (Tim and Alice)

Filled Potential (Ty and Juniper)

Fragile Illusion (Thatcher and Emma)

A Stag Family Christmas

Beautiful Game (Hawk and Lucy)

Stag Generations Series

Forging Passion (Wes and Cara prequel)

Forging Glory (Wes and Cara)

Forging Legacy (coming soon)

Forging Chaos (coming soon)

Stone Creek University

Deep in the Pocket: A Football Romance

Hard Edge: A Hockey Romance

Possession: A Football Romance

* 9 7 8 1 9 5 7 1 4 5 5 0 1 *